ONCE U͜PON A HORSE

BOOK THREE

THE ONCE UPON A HORSE SERIES

THE FLYING HORSE

THE JOCKEY & HER HORSE

THE STAR HORSE

ONCE UPON A HORSE

THE STAR HORSE

BY SARAH MASLIN NIR

art by LAYLIE FRAZIER

cameron kids

Book design by Melissa Nelson Greenberg
Edited by Summer Dawn Laurie

Library of Congress Control Number: 2023947383
ISBN: 978-1-951836-68-9
eISBN: 979-8-88707-345-3

Printed in the U.S.A.

10 9 8 7 6 5 4 3 2 1

CAMERON KIDS books are available at special discounts when purchased in
quantity for premiums and promotions as well as fundraising or educational
use. Special editions can also be created to specifications. For details, contact
specialsales@abramsbooks.com or the address below.

ABRAMS The Art of Books
195 Broadway, New York, NY 10007
abramsbooks.com

To the riders and horses of
GallopNYC—you are stars.

—SMN

PROLOGUE

In the center of the most glittering city in the entire world is a spot that shines even more brightly. Six low steps lead to a fountain. Along the edge of each stair run ribbons of light upon which blink hundreds of illuminated words. You will know you are in New York City, the heart of the world, where people from all lands live, by what you read on those stairs: *Salut*, *Yōkoso*, *Khush Aamdeed*, *Bienvenido*, and more. *Welcome* glows in all the languages under the sun.

The fountain, a pool of glimmering water in a circle of granite that shines like the eye of a cat at night, swishes and swirls. Three hundred and fifty-three jets spout water, and every few minutes they send up plumes of liquid sixty feet into the air! When the droplets come sparkling back down, the water below dances. The building that lies beyond the fountain twinkles from underneath five arches of cream-colored limestone. A warm glow bounces through windows that are as clear as day but crisscrossed like the stained glass of a church.

Stand here, in this magic spot called Lincoln Center, and you behold beauty with more than just your eyes. Listen! Beyond the fountain, across the limestone, and through the thick glass you will hear something special. It is the hint of a song, the melody of an orchestra, and the tuning of a symphony. Music is everywhere here, warming everything it touches, like sunlight shining across a landscape. That is because up those steps, past that fountain, and under those arches is the Metropolitan Opera, the grandest stage in the world.

Now imagine if you happened to see all this and hear all this, *and* you were a little yellow horse from

Norway. A horse who suddenly found himself standing before the majestic sight of Lincoln Center. You might understandably have butterflies in your horsey tummy.

"It's OK, Billy," Lori Allegria said to the tubby blond animal at her elbow, as they stood before the fountain. The horse had begun to tremble a little.

Billy was a type of equine known as a Norwegian Fjord horse. Like almost all his relatives, he was sandy colored and smallish, more rightly a pony than a horse. Ponies are not baby horses; they are simply shorter than fourteen hands and two inches at the shoulder. Any equine that is taller is a horse. *Hands?* That's the unique way these animals are measured, a unit of measurement first used way back in ancient Egypt. Look at your palm. It's likely about four or so inches across. A *hand* is four inches long. Billy was *almost* a pony. He was fourteen hands and two inches and a smidge. Most people saw him and thought, *Aww, cute pony*. But he thought of himself as a big, strapping horse.

Like all of his herd, he had a jet-black ribbon of fur running from the tip of his ears to the end of his bushy tail, tracing a path down his spine. This is called a dorsal stripe, and nearly every Fjord has one running along their back. It is set off starkly against the blond hair of their body, as if a writer stroked each animal with an inky quill.

Lori ran her soft hand through the puff of black hair on Billy's forehead, using her fingers to comb straight the fluffy tuft between his eyes called a forelock. Billy stopped shivering. The seventh grader made him his bran mash every day at the farm where he now lived in a town called Springs. It was a small, sandy town in the shadow of New York City. She was the person who mixed in a dollop of molasses with the warm water and bran flakes so that it was a touch sweet, just as he liked. Secretly (so the other horses at the farm, a Clydesdale and a thoroughbred, would not see and know she was playing favorites), she sliced up apples just for him, too, and plopped them in the mash. Granny Smiths only, just as he preferred. Billy loved to snuffle through his porridge and find the extracrunchy treat.

Billy and Lori were the same age. The same week Tessa brought Lori home from the hospital, she bought a present for her healthy baby girl. With the savings she built during her first year at the law firm, Tessa purchased Billy, a tiny weanling, which means he had just stopped drinking mare's milk. Looking out the window at the foal grazing while rocking baby Lori in her arms, the new mother was proud of what she could provide for her daughter, all on her own. And so, the newborn and the foal grew up together on the farm in Springs, a herd of two.

As herd animals, Billy and all equines get their information about danger and safety from other members of their herd, human or horse. There at Lincoln Center, Lori's calm demeanor and joyful face told him he was still safe, even in all the strangeness. If Lori liked this dazzling place she had brought him to—even with its freaky fountain that did *not* behave like the water in his trough at home—well, then he would try to like it too.

All around the little horse, people were hurrying across the great flagstones of the plaza in which he stood. Some were dressed in sumptuous silks, the trains of their gowns swishing like horse tails as the ladies slipped around the fountain. The people glittered like the dancing water, light bouncing off jewels around necks and on cuff links. It even glinted on the shiny surface of a dapper top hat or two. To Billy, the people looked almost like a herd of horses in the summer sun, they *gleamed* so. The herd of people were all heading in one direction, toward the five great arches of the Metropolitan Opera.

It is not very usual to see a horse at the theater. But it is not so *un*usual to see things you've never, ever seen in New York City. So, the onrushing people did not stare at the blond equine as much as you'd have thought. A lot happens in that big, thrumming place of art and commerce and busyness and dreams, and there's a lot to pay attention to. So sometimes things really *worth* taking the time to see—like a brave little horse's trust in the girl he loves, a thing so powerful you could almost see it glowing between the two if you actually took the time to *really* look—are missed. In their haste to get inside the Met, to get on with their own journeys, the fabulously dressed people mostly missed witnessing an incredible journey just beginning there beside the fountain. A few turned rouge-painted cheeks and kohl-smoked eyes in Lori and Billy's direction—but only for a moment. One woman raised a penciled eyebrow at the sight, then hustled on.

But one top-hatted person stopped. He was a boy of about twelve. If anyone had been paying attention to anything beyond the ends of their own noses that night, they would have thought it unusual that such a young boy was so finely dressed. He was in a tuxedo with two tails that flicked out like a swallow's. His head was under a miniature version of those felted top hats that the most dashing of grown men were wearing that night. The boy stopped. He tipped back his top hat. Then he peered intently at the pair on the plaza.

In that moment, he thought he saw that secret something between girl and horse. Actually, he felt it. Then he felt a tug on his silken sleeve. "Marlowe!

The reporters are waiting for you on the red carpet," a man in a wheelchair said to the boy. Beside him was a big black Labrador retriever. The dog was wearing a bow tie, just like the boy! Marlowe tore his eyes away from Billy and Lori and followed his friend in the wheelchair and the sweet black Lab into the big amber building.

Lori did not notice the boy. She had eyes only for her horse, and her thoughts were only of comforting him, of helping him feel brave. The little horse was frankly starstruck. He was staring skyward at all the glitter. When he finally pulled his focus away from all the lights, it was to nose around Lori's pocket in case she had any apple slices hiding there.

A snack would be just the thing to calm his nerves, he was sure.

"Billy, what you're feeling is only natural," Lori told him, petting the black-tipped edges of his yellow ears. She pulled out a baggie from her pocket and slipped him some slices of green Granny Smith apple. They both knew horses and ponies could not understand human language. But Lori felt it was the right thing to do to at least *try* to explain this unusual situation to the little horse. She wished she could tell him so much! Starting with why she and her mother had put him on the trailer that morning and trucked him from the quiet Long Island town where he lived to bustling New York City.

And that he was about to become a star.

Chapter 1

THE MAESTRO

It had all happened so fast.

It was just a day ago that Lori had fizzled with excitement as she stood in exactly the same place, Lincoln Center—without the little horse. Instead, she had been surrounded by her classmates at Springs Middle School, all on a class trip from their small town to the Metropolitan Opera. During that block of history class, the seventh graders were studying ancient Egypt. They had learned about the goddesses and gods, like Isis, who reigned over the Nile River, and Ra, the sun king. They had learned about hieroglyphics, the ancient Egyptian form of writing, and Lori practiced "horse" until it was perfect. They

had learned about hands, the ancient Egyptian unit of measurement. (Though Lori had known all about *that* already, having been born on a farm and used to measuring ponies and horses, counting four-inch increments right up to where their shoulder blades met, a spot called the withers.)

Now it was field trip day—to ancient Egypt! Well, sort of. As fun as it would be to travel back in time, since time machines had yet to be invented, the class did the next best thing: The students were at Lincoln Center to see a rehearsal of *Aida*, an opera written by nineteenth-century Italian composer Giuseppe Verdi and set in an imaginary version of ancient Egypt. Even better was a fact that had Lori bouncing on the balls of her feet just thinking about it: The whole grade had backstage passes! The special trip had been made possible by her mother, a lawyer who helped the opera with legal stuff like contracts for its vast cast.

Lori's mother had taken the day off work to chaperone the school trip. That was a difficult task, Lori knew. Her mother, Tessa, worked weekdays, weeknights, and even some weekends at her law firm to afford to keep the family farm she'd grown up on in Springs. Recently they'd taken on boarders, a Clydesdale named BonBon and a thoroughbred named Express Lane (Elaine for short), to help pay the bills. She'd chosen to have Lori on her own, so raising her daughter *and* keeping the farm afloat was all on Tessa. She kept a happy face about it. But from time to time, Lori overheard conversations with bill collectors—the feed man and the hay man and the shavings man—demanding her mother pay overdue bills *or else*. She knew their idyllic life on the farm was precarious.

But today was a special class trip, and she was grateful her mother had taken the time to be there with her, even if it cost her. Along with the teachers, her mom helped herd the seventh graders across the plaza, past the grand arched entrance, through a small green door in the side of the building. It creaked open, and waiting for them was the opera conductor himself!

"Ms. Allegria! My *esteemed* guests!" he said, flourishing his hands and making a little bow as the class giggled at such formality. "My name is Alfonso Vélez, but you may call me *Maestro*—it means 'conductor' in Italian, the most operatic language of all." All at once, the maestro straightened up, soldierlike, and threw his arms wide. "Welcome to ancient Egypt!"

The class poured into a treasure trove rarely seen by any of the people who sit in their fine clothes on the other side of the curtain and watch the performance. Backstage was an entire Egyptian city! It was filled with extraordinary props. Jewels and amulets hung in rows from hooks on a wall. Tablets etched with hieroglyphs were piled in a corner. Golden shields and fearsome spears leaned in rows against a wall—the Egyptian army's weapons. There were columns that looked like they had come straight from the Temple of Isis, but when the conductor rapped one with his knuckles as they passed . . . *clunk*! It was not solid sandstone but hollow papier-mâché. As the students peered around, Ms. Allegria fished some final contracts from her bag. Maestro leaned against a statue of a sphynx (also papier-mâché) to sign them as he asked the seventh graders to gather before him. The maestro hooked his pinky around a warrior's spear that was leaning against the column and picked it up—it wasn't metal at all; it was light as a feather!

"The magic of the theater," he said with a laugh at their surprised gasps. "This is a world of *pretend*." As he showed them this and that, actors filed in, gathering for rehearsal, half dressed in their costumes; Lori giggled at all the things that no one would have seen in the *real* ancient Egypt: hot-pink workout pants underneath a toga. One actor wore a loincloth—over blue jeans. "Never mind my frumpily dressed cast!" the maestro said loudly, brandishing the contracts,

and the actors warming up for that night's performance within earshot chuckled in response. "Every
costume detail you see here—minus the dungarees,
of course, but they will be *banished* by showtime—is
historically accurate, the work of extensive research
into everything ancient Egyptian—just like I hear
your grade has been doing," he said. "So, minus
the fact that the spears are plastic and the shields
are Styrofoam, everything *looks* just as we believe it
would have beside the Nile. From the weapons to
the headdresses, everything is as it was—even the
costumes for the horses."

"*HORSES?*" Lori burst out from where she sat on
the backstage floor.

She quickly clapped her hand over her mouth. Every
eye in the cavernous space turned to look at her,
even the maestro's. But *his* eyes had a strange look
of . . . frustration? Sadness? "Yes, in this world of
pretend, productions of *Aida* around the world send
a *real-life horse* across the stage, bearing the com-
mander of the Egyptian army." He closed his eyes

and clasped his hands over his heart in a theatrical swoon. "Oh, children, Verdi's music swells around them, and there's nothing so magnificent in all of theater." His face crumpled suddenly. "But I'm afraid here, that part of the show will not go on," the maestro said, punctuating his speech with a heavy sigh. He turned to Lori's mother. "Ms. Allegria, you are so, so good with my contracts, the whole corps is set, the ballerinas and the baritones." He slumped where he stood. "But I am still missing the most important cast member!"

Lori cocked her head. There were hundreds of people backstage, flitting about, stretching, rehearsing, jabbing fake spears at one another. Who could be missing?

"A horse! A horse, my kingdom for a horse!" the maestro said, crumpling the contracts in his hands before Lori's mom could stop him and waving them in a flourish. "The Egyptian army captain—Princess Aida's secret love—must ride in from battle on a real, live horse!" he cried, his voice rising in exasperation.

He smushed the papers to his forehead as Ms. Allegria tried to snatch them back and save the documents, and the children sat back a bit on the floor. The maestro was having a meltdown.

"But you tell me, where can I find an *actual* horse to star in an opera in New York City!"

Lori was a shy child. She spent most of her time speaking to the horses on the farm where she lived in Springs, quietly whispering into their manes about what happened at school that day, reading them book reports, or showing them her geometry homework. At school she had a hard time speaking up. That was in part because she felt awkward. Lori felt awkward because she was tall. Very tall. It had happened the summer before sixth grade, when all of a sudden, she noticed her heels nearly dangling past Billy's belly when she rode him. Now, the seventh grader was taller than her teacher, Ms. Trachtman! Everyone assumed she played basketball or volleyball, not rode horses. Sometimes they called her "Mrs. Lori" like *she* was a teacher. When that happened, she wanted to sink through the ground. Or shrink! Of course, in reality, Lori had zero reason to be anything but proud of who she was, whatever shape she took. We are all different. It would be so boring otherwise. So are horses. Horses never care who is as tall as Sampson, the shaggy shire gelding who was born in 1846 in England and grew to be a whopping world-record twenty-one-and-a-half hands high! Or who is a miniature Falabella horse no bigger than a Labrador retriever. To one another, they're all horses, different in some ways but alike in what matters: horsiness.

Lori should have learned that lesson from her tubby Fjord horse. Billy, like all horses, stood proud next to the lanky thoroughbred, Elaine, and the strapping Clydesdale, BonBon, on her family farm. If Lori had paid attention, she might have learned to stand tall in who she was. Instead, she stooped, slumped, and slouched to make herself less tall. When seventh grade began, she tried a drastic new tactic to be a little less visible: staying quiet. It often made her sad not to say what was on her mind. But she felt so awkward in her body when she was mistaken for a teacher and so embarrassed when asked to come to the front of the class to pull down the projector screen. Staying quiet soothed those nerves.

But, when it came to her best friend, her Norwegian Fjord horse, and her mother, who looked so distressed as the maestro neared tears, she couldn't stay quiet. Maybe she could help.

Lori spoke up.

"Maestro," Lori said, swallowing her bashfulness as all the other seventh graders swiveled their heads toward her unexpected interruption. She stood up from the floor and forgot for a moment her fear of towering over others. She cleared her throat and found her courage.

"I think I need to introduce you to a family member of mine. His name is Billy."

Chapter 2

AIDA

The next day Billy and Lori had woken up before dawn at the farm in Springs and, as usual, had breakfast together. Lori sat on a hay bale in the stables and enjoyed a blueberry muffin. Beside her in his stall, Billy slurped up his sweet morning mash of wheat bran with a touch of molasses. She'd even fed Billy a muffin crumb. She'd laughed as he curled up his lip and wrinkled his nose, a funny face she had learned from the local vet was called a flehmen response. Horses rumple their muzzles when they taste something unfamiliar. But for the rest of the day, nothing was "as usual."

Billy had gotten the part in the opera!

After much discussion of Lori's "inspired!" idea and more paper signing with the maestro, it was agreed that Billy would fill in for the role of the warrior's horse. The little Fjord horse could save the opera! That morning was a blur. Her mother had written to her teacher at Springs Middle for special permission to take the day off from school. But even free from first-period computer science class, Lori worked hard that morning: She groomed Billy's coat with a curry-comb, working in circles to loosen any dust. Then she brushed him all over with a stiff brush and finally a polishing soft brush. She combed out all the tangles in his black-and-yellow mane. With a hoof pick, she cleaned out any dirt in his hooves. On the underside, she was careful to avoid the sensitive triangle at the center of his hoof with the funny name—"frog"—that the veterinarian had taught her is actually a horse's toe.

When she was done, it seemed to her that the gold in Billy's coat flared as brightly as the chandeliers of the theater.

Lori led him onto the trailer and secured him in the stall with a bar across his chest. It was a horsey seat belt for the hours-long journey to New York City. All the while she told him about her past visit to Lincoln Center, about opera, about music, about the grand orchestra, and about the diva, the powerful female singer playing the starring role of Aida whom he was about to meet.

But even if Billy could have understood his girl Lori's excited chattering, little could have prepared him for what he was about to experience. He had never been to a city. And he certainly had never been to an opera.

Showtime. Lincoln Center. The glitter. The glow.

"It's called stage fright," Lori said to him after he at last stepped off the trailer and they stood by the fountain at Lincoln Center. There were no stalls backstage at the Metropolitan Opera, of course, so animal actors arrived *just* before the curtain rose and took their positions. "That's all you're feeling.

It will pass." He stopped quaking. She tugged his lead rope gently and drew him past the five arches to a small green door that led backstage. Billy swiveled his black-tipped ears—each of which could turn 180 degrees and move independently—and suddenly caught a wonderful sound.

He had never heard anything like it. Drums and violins, flutes and harps, and trumpets and trombones, echoed from just behind the five arches of the grand building before them. Billy did not know what made the extraordinary sound, of course. The horse was only familiar with the sounds of his world: the snuffling of horses, the crowing of roosters, and the lowing of cows. But he knew he *loved it*. As he listened to the music, the butterflies that had seemed to fill the horse's tummy fluttered away. They were replaced by something else: excitement. The green door creaked open.

"Billy," Lori whispered into his soot-tipped ear. "You're going to be a star."

Billy sniffed the air and curled his nose again in his funny flehmen smile. He'd loved the smells of his barn—the hay, the fresh grass, the soft woodchips. But nothing was as intoxicating as the smells, sounds, and sights of this new world: backstage. He almost trotted through.

All around him were actors, hundreds of them, dressed in flowing robes and carrying faux spears and shields. They were the Egyptian army of *Aida*. They wielded shields that looked massive but turned out to be Styrofoam and silver paint, just props— light enough so that the actors could dance and twirl with their battle gear. Lori was beside him as a prop master gently draped a blanket painted the same silver over Billy's back. It hung with tassels and jingled when he moved. His friend stroked under his chin and at the top of his forelock, where the black stripe blended into his gold. Billy wished he could tell her he wasn't frightened anymore; it was all just a *thrill* to him. They stepped across the stage to their places, behind a curtain of gold. Almost showtime.

Plink PLINK plink!

A xylophone rang out. Everyone around him seemed to know what the three tones meant: Places, everyone! The show was about to begin! Standing with Billy behind the golden curtain, the prop master drew out a final touch from his box of costumes: a drooping ostrich plume. He handed it to Lori. She raised the feather above the top of the horse's head right between his ears, which is called a poll. She poked it into the crownpiece of his bridle. Billy eyed the feather suspiciously as it bobbed above his head. "Billy, this ostrich plume is an honor. When you wear it on your head, it means you are a warrior horse!"

The strong tones of his girl's voice made him feel brave, whatever it was she was saying. He puffed out his chest and raised his wedge-shaped head, exactly like a warrior horse would!

"What a specimen you've got here, Lori!" It was the maestro, alongside the actor playing the Egyptian army captain. It was moments until the curtain would rise. "We'll take it from here, my young horse-woman. I'm fairly certain there were no Springs Middle School students in ancient Egypt, so you'd better duck offstage."

Before Lori slipped to stage left, out of sight in the wings, she pulled out her baggie of apple pieces and pressed the stash into the actor's palm. "In case he gets stage fright," she whispered. The man smiled and tucked the snack into a fold of his sarong as he took the Fjord horse's reins.

As the golden curtain rose, Billy soared with excitement. The music crescendoed, the drums and violins, flutes and harps, and trumpets and trombones. The ostrich plume dove and swayed, his golden hide glittered, and his smokey stripe gleamed. When the audience caught sight of the magnificent little horse, there in the middle of New York City, onstage, they were no longer blasé city folk who had seen *everything*. They were starstruck. When the applause began, it washed over him more warmly than a currycomb. He shivered with delight at the sound.

The little horse was so thrilled, so impressed with himself, that for one of the first times in his life, Billy hardly noticed Lori was not at his side.

Chapter 3

WHINNY

Marlowe Narang sat stiffly, even in his cushy red velvet seat. He wore a custom tuxedo, and the beauty of the fancy stitching that scrolled along the lapels and traced the edge of the collar could not make up for the fact that it *itched*. Twelve-year-olds didn't normally wear designer duds, but Marlowe was not a normal preteen. He was a celebrity.

And right then, seated in the front row of the grand opera house of Lincoln Center, Marlowe was *hating* that fact.

He had just shuffled in from the Lincoln Center courtyard, past the fountain, past the girl and the horse who had briefly captivated him, and past a gaggle of reporters calling out his name. "Pthhhhhbt!" He let out a spluttering, world-weary sigh, one that you'd usually hear from someone five times his age. At his feet, the black Lab with the bow tie pricked her ears in concern.

Normally it was a pretty fun life, if a little unusual. These days he lived in Los Angeles, California, in a boxy white house from which he could see the Pacific Ocean through a stand of palm trees, tipped sideways by the salty breeze.

His career had begun four years earlier. With a dog food commercial! Marlowe could still recite the lines he had chirped into the prying eye of a video camera for a "screen test" when he was eight years old. His mother and father, Fatima and Fred, owned a shoe store in Bullhead City, Arizona, a town at the edge of the Mojave Desert where Marlowe grew up. The store was called Fatima's Feet and had been his mother's idea. She *adored* shoes and tried on every single one she put up for sale. That day as he and his mother walked back to the store after school, they passed a woman holding a camera. In an offhand way, she called to them: "Hey, kid, want to try out for a dog food commercial?"

They had no idea that moment would change their lives forever—does anyone know when fate and luck take over and your path is about to diverge dramatically from the life you expected? That camerawoman's question launched Marlowe toward Hollywood fame.

Perhaps it was better that Marlowe and Fatima didn't recognize this moment as so pivotal, or there would have been pressure to perform perfectly. That, as everyone knows, is a recipe for stress. Instead, it seemed a grand game to mother and son—to be asked to recite some lines about doggy kibble into a camera, what fun! So, when the lady pointed the lens at his small face, Marlowe delivered the words with an impish giggle.

"Love your pup?" little Marlowe had recited, there on Bullhead City's Main Street. His dark eyes glittered into a camera lens almost the size of his head. "But are you sure he loves you back?" He lowered his lashes, filled with grief as he imagined his father's own Labrador, Blue, not loving him back. The thought darkened his brow and made his eyes sheen with real sadness. "Feed him Khoury's Kibble, and you won't have to guess!" *Wink!* Marlowe's chin went up, and the lady behind the camera, with his mother beside her, brightened with him as his round face beamed with his internal joy. It was the first glimpse at what Marlowe's acting could do to his audience and what would soon make him a star: Marlowe could make people *feel.*

Just then, a familiar man in a wheelchair passed by the impromptu audition, a black Lab trotting beside him in a navy service dog vest. It was Fred, Marlowe's dad, and Blue. "Oh my, I've got to get some of that Khoury's Kibble for my Blue," he called to his son. He pulled his electric wheelchair to a stop beside them so swiftly that the tires made a little squeak on the pavement. "With a pitch like that, I'm sold!"

The lady took her eye off her camera's scope. She seemed to recognize Fred and glared at him. Hurriedly, she pulled out a sheaf of papers from a satchel slung over her shoulder and fished a pen out from the bottom of the bag. She did not address Fred or Marlowe, but Fatima instead. "Ma'am," she said. "Your kid's got the part for Khoury's Kibble if you want it." His mother's mouth fell open a little. She took the papers—a contract for Marlowe's first commercial acting gig—and her eyes bumped back and forth as she read the legal language carefully.

"Do not sign a *thing!*" Fred boomed, his dog suddenly sitting down at the commotion, alert for anything that may need doing.

Marlowe's mother popped her eyes up from the paper. "But, Fred, this woman said our son is *a natural*," she said.

The woman with the camera gasped in surprise: "'Our' son? You're Fred Narang, aren't you?" she said slowly, as you could see the connections click in her head. "This is your kid?" she exclaimed, her eyes narrowing to slits. "*The* Hollywood agent responsible for landing half the movie deals of the 1990s? I heard you disappeared from Hollywood a decade ago." She slapped her thigh. "Ugh! Just my luck, this is *your* kid."

Fred smiled. "You heard right. I did disappear. I came to this town to raft the Colorado River, needed a little break—agent life didn't suit me. I got me a special raft that accommodates me and even my girl Blue," he said. "That 'little break' became permanent: got swept away rafting—by my nature guide, a Bullhead City woman who just *adores* shoes." He winked at Fatima.

"But, Marlowe." Fred turned to his son. "For you, I could un-retire for a bit. I was hoping to keep that talent under my own roof for a bit longer." Fred smiled as Blue thumped her tail. "But there's no hiding your gift anymore. You could sell *anyone* that dog food—even a *cat*!" Marlowe beamed.

Fred reached out and took the papers from his wife's hand. "I'm better at selling shoes these days, but I still remember how to read a Hollywood contract—and make sure no one is getting hustled." The woman crossed her arms and scoffed. "We'll look it over as a family and get back to you," Fred told her. She walked off in a huff.

So from a bit of luck and some dog kibble, Marlowe Narang, the current coolest boy in Hollywood, was minted. That serendipity on the streets of Bullhead City, getting the Khoury's Kibble commercial, was just the start. That commercial ran on every television station and in every YouTube video opener for over nine months. Marlowe's face (right beside a cute puppy, of course) was plastered on every bag of Khoury's Kibble, and he became known as the Kibble Kid.

Soon he was advertising cereal and sneakers, rental cars and rice crackers. By the time fourth grade rolled around, he was busy with so many gigs, or acting jobs, that he stopped attending Coyote Canyon Elementary School in Bullhead City, and Fred took over his son's tutoring on the road. As predicted that day on Main Street, Fred unretired, but this time around, being a Hollywood agent was much more fun: Father, son, and service dog traveled from set to set, together. Back in Bullhead City, Fatima tried on each new shoe as the inventory came in, running the store to support Marlowe's career (all those flights to auditions had to be paid for!). In his absence, she daydreamed about which pair she'd strut down the red carpet in when her son won his first Oscar. For Fred, watching the joy Marlowe got from every line, every camera, and every request for his autograph made saying goodbye for a time to the shoe shop and Fatima a little easier.

But no one was ever ready for a final goodbye. Marlowe's star had been rising for more than a year when Fatima fell gravely ill. As she battled through cancer, Fred and Marlowe left the middle of a shoot for a new brand of vanilla bean pudding to be by her side. Fatima would have none of it. She wanted him back out there on set, doing what he loved. "Honey, you know what I love?"

Marlowe giggled a little as he knelt by her bedside back in Bullhead City. "Heels! Pumps! Flip-flops!" he rattled off.

"No," she said, drawing him back to seriousness. "I love *you*. It was my dream to have a shoe shop. To have a partner like your father. But most of all to have you." She reached over and tousled his hair. "You are all my dreams come true." Her eyes crinkled with a quiet smile. "I want you to keep my dream alive by going after yours." Marlowe buried his head in his shirtsleeve then, thinking the unthinkable: a world in which his mother wasn't there dreaming alongside him.

"But, Marlowe," she continued. He looked up again. "It is not enough that we follow our own dreams. Why do I work every day in this shoe shop? It ain't just for the loafers, honey! So I can help you reach for the stars. Life is about helping others realize their dreams too."

Fatima passed away just after Marlowe finished fourth grade. Marlowe threw himself even more deeply into acting. In part, it was to follow his mother's wish for him, but there was something else driving him: He loved the feeling of becoming someone else for a moment, whether a puppy chow "spokeskid" or a frosted oats salesboy. When he was them, he was not the person he was offstage: a boy without a mom. He did not have to think about the day Fred closed Fatima's Feet, helping tug the iron window grate down for the last time. His father couldn't bear to be around all the beautiful shoes his wife had loved, without its namesake trying on each one and strutting around the shop floor with a laugh.

When the television shows came calling, it was an easy decision for father and son to leave Bullhead City behind. "Would Marlowe like to have a walk-on part?" the directors asked Fred. Their town beside the Colorado River echoed with Fatima, how she was strong and fierce when guiding backpackers through the desert or along the rapids and soft and silly modeling espadrilles and slingbacks. Hollywood would be a fresh start. Fred threw himself into being Marlowe's agent, far from his shoe store full of memories. Marlowe also chucked himself headlong into Tinseltown, driven by a desire to forget who he was. "Would Marlowe like to have his own show?" Soon those bit parts became starring roles.

By the time Marlowe was seated in that soft red velvet seat in that fabulous but *so, so itchy* suit in the very front row at the Metropolitan Opera at Lincoln Center, he'd been a working actor for four whole years. His father worked full time as an agent for just him, making sure he got the best gigs, tallying his paychecks, and balancing the twelve-year-old's bank accounts. He felt proud to have given his father a new purpose and to shine in roles in honor of his mother, who had loved nothing more than for him to dream aloud onstage.

And yet. Four years on, he was getting tired of being a celebrity. The "child star" stuff was a lot more than just throwing himself into being another person in front of a camera. He loved *acting*, but the promotion required for each role—interviews, photo shoots, appearances at dog food expos—was tiring and so time-consuming. Yes, it all came with special treatment like limos, private jets, and adoring fans, but by then, Marlowe had started to take it for granted. And once you stop appreciating what you have, whether it's the opportunity to sit in the front row at the premiere of the grandest opera in the world or whether it's realizing simply how lucky you are to have a roof to sleep under when so many people don't—that's when things start to go wrong.

There at the opera, Marlowe crossed his arms, slumped down into in his red velvet seat, and was so preoccupied by his inner storm that he barely heard the music swell. Above his head, twelve crystal chandeliers shaped like starbursts slipped upward on golden chains until the light fixtures were tucked high underneath the vaulted ceiling and the light dimmed. Marlowe didn't notice.

Blue's tail thumped; the Labrador could tell that Fred was brimming with joy in the beautiful theater. Fatima would have loved it here, the music, the acting—the fabulous shoes. And memories of her made his heart swell. Fred's happiness made his dog happy, as it does for all animals whose owners are kindly and good.

Marlowe didn't see.

Above them soared a ceiling covered in sheets of delicate twenty-three-karat gold leaf. It was designed so that the tiniest tinkling of a cymbal could be heard across the whole theater. It amplified every note, every sound, and sent the music right into the heart of every listener.

Marlowe stared at his navel.

As the lights went dark, an unhappy thought slid into his mind. In the glitz and glamour, the autograph lines and ribbon cuttings, had he lost his ability to dream? At the edge of the stage in front of him, the maestro raised his conductor's baton, and the drums and violins, flutes and harps, trumpets and trombones began to sound. Marlowe was so lost in thought he could hardly hear the exquisite symphony. He had loved acting, but for a while now, he'd lost hold of what he once saw reflected in his mother's eyes.

Then the golden curtain rose.

"*A HORSE!*" Marlowe yelped into the vast theater, before he could control himself. He clapped his hand over his mouth. Fred and Blue startled beside him. At the loud sound, so close to where he stood center stage, Billy's head shot up. With the spotlights shining into his eyes, the horse could not see a single one of the thousands of red velvet seats in the audience. Marlowe's unexpected squawk, so close to his hooves, sounded a lot like—a wolf? A jackal? A mountain lion? *Something that eats horses?* Billy's mind raced.

For a moment Billy did not do anything other than stand rigid in fear. Then the small horse drew in a breath, puffing up his chest. He raised his muzzle. He unleashed an equine alarm: a wild, bugling *WHINNY!* It bounced off the twenty-three-karat ceiling and made the crystal in the twenty-one chandeliers hum with its vibration. It was sharper—and some would later say more beautiful—than any instrument of the orchestra. With it, his nostrils flared, his hooves planted, Billy went from fluffy Norwegian horse with a feather on his head to a steed fit for a true warrior.

The audience whispered in their velvet seats, *"What a star!"* The reporters scribbled in their notebooks, *What a star.* Lori thought from behind the curtain, *What a star.* And Marlowe said to his dad, "I want that horse in my next movie."

Chapter 4

ONCE UPON A HORSE

That night Lori couldn't sleep. She tossed and turned in her bed in Springs. It wasn't the next day's vocabulary test keeping her up. She had tried studying her flash cards until she became dizzy. But she was so distracted she couldn't memorize anything past "A."

Adulation, noun, *excessive praise*

Appall, verb, *to horrify or greatly dismay*

Astonishing, adjective, *extremely impressive, amazing*

She put the beat-up flash cards on her nightstand and pressed her lashes together. The dazzling lights of the opera, the shimmering splashes of the fountain, and the sweeping music of the orchestra exploded behind her lids. She was overwhelmed by the kaleidoscope of art and light she had witnessed hours before. In her bedroom back on the farm, Lori had a vision. She was leading her little horse from behind the golden curtains. But when they rose, it wasn't the Fjord who pranced and performed. *She* was performing. Under the covers she danced a pas de deux with the Egyptian army captain. Then she *was* the warrior. Next, she stood center stage and belted out an aria. She was an opera diva!

Yet as soon as these spectacular thoughts spangled the insides of her eyelids, she stopped them. She pulled the coverlet up to her chin and huddled more deeply beneath it, suddenly scared. How could she dare to have such wild dreams? Lori, who didn't like when people looked at her? (And they *always* looked at her: head and shoulders above everyone in her class picture; on field trips when she was mistaken for a chaperone; when substitute teachers thought she was a colleague. Ugh!) But she loved learning new things, whether they be new skills, new words, or new ways of moving. As the fall breeze played with her gauze curtains, an echo of the golden velvet that had thrilled her, she opened her eyes and grabbed her flash cards again. Adulation . . . appall. She let out a little huff of air as she read the card once again. The stage, for someone as gawky and out of place as her? How could Lori, who felt she never fit in anywhere, dream of being a member of something as seamless as the great glittering corps of a cast? The audience, Lori was sure, would be *appalled*.

If Billy or anyone else who loved Lori had been able to hear these unkind thoughts she was having about herself, they would have seriously corrected her. For what is more interesting than difference? What else makes life fascinating and curious and special than the ways in which we each add our individuality to the great project that is life on planet Earth? How boring if every horse was dusty yellow with a black dorsal stripe like Billy—even as cute as he was? There is beauty in the mosaic of bay and chestnut and dapple gray and pinto and palomino and buckskin in a herd of thoroughbreds galloping over fields toward breakfast. Horses' delightful differences go far deeper than fur: Some ponies pull milk carts through the streets of Austria; some horses haul bricks to build the houses of Senegal. Even the prancing Lipizzaner stallions of Vienna, who all grow up snow white, each have their own unique way of dancing on air.

Outside, past the whir of cicadas in the hayfields, Billy was sleepless as well. The little horse lay with his tufted heels folded under him, his whiskered chin resting in the soft pine that was his bed. His nostrils were blowing curls of shavings to and fro as he thought through the adventure that had been his day. Usually, his most exciting days were when he raced through the woods with Lori on his back. She would giggle as he leapt logs with extra oomph. (He always tried to jump with zing just to hear that sound.) But his time onstage had been different. In the barn, he could almost feel the stroke of each violin bow through his yellow coat. The strum of harp strings played across his flanks. The scales of the xylophone seemed to comb through his mane. It was the shattering applause that kept him wakeful most of all. The thundering of handclaps had felt like Lori patting the crest of his neck for a job well done . . . times a million! Until that night at the opera, Billy had lived for nothing more than the love of his girl and the crunch of Granny Smith apple slices. Now, he had found something more delicious. He didn't have a word for it. But up at the farmhouse on a grubby notecard on Lori's bedside table was exactly what the little horse was thinking about and savoring: adulation.

What had swept through his fur and right down to his bones was the delicious feeling of being absolutely adored. Thousands of people had told him, "Good horse, Billy!" just as Lori, his one girl, did every day. (And really every few minutes, she loved him so, and he really was very, very good, as are all horses.) It was that very same praise amplified. It had bounced off the starburst-shaped chandeliers. Hovered over every red velvet seat. And it had cascaded across the front of the stage, or proscenium, where he had stood. It had flooded the Fjord horse until all that adoration, that *adulation*, felt like it would shoot straight out of his spiky mane and down the ink-black dorsal stripe along the length of his spine. The fluttering applause seemed to continue there in the quiet barn, filling his stall, pouring out of the manger, and washing around in his water buckets. It replayed over and over in the little equine's mind. It was better than apples. When he finally rested that night Billy knew one thing: he wanted more.

If the horse and the girl had not been so completely consumed with their thoughts that night, they might have heard the muted roar of a small private plane. The Cessna was like a limo in the sky. It held just two passengers and one sleepy dog wearing a bow tie. Blue was very used to flying in private jets around the world by then. She helped Fred navigate crowded airport terminals in his wheelchair. She cleared a path by walking in front of him in her service-dog vest as he flew from movie premieres to red-carpet awards shows. She could retrieve items like his passport and ticket gently in her muzzle if he accidentally dropped them on the floor. She was even trained to push elevator buttons with her nose if Fred could not reach. Blue was off the clock now, sprawled out in a doggy bed, her paws wiggling as she dreamed. Fred snored a little, too, as the Cessna and his family made their way back to Hollywood.

Marlowe was not asleep. He was as wide-eyed as a newborn foal taking in the world. There was so much to think about and plan. He stared out the window at New York City receding below, its dazzling lights becoming pinpricks beneath him. The plane turned west for California, away from Springs, its stables and farmhouses turning dollhouse-sized as the plane gained altitude.

It was six hours to Los Angeles, and for the entire journey Marlowe Narang did not sleep a wink. He'd whipped off the itchy tuxedo as soon as the opera ended and was now in comfy soft sweatpants and a hoodie. Marlowe thought about the adorable golden horse with the plume on his head. The horse had shone—every part of him had, from his hooves to his forelock. Marlowe knew that glow. It was that same feeling he'd gotten when he first started acting: like every dream was possible. When you're in exactly the place you're meant to be, that feeling wraps you up like a downy duvet. It has a name—fulfillment— and so many people look for it in the wrong places. For Marlowe, the joy of simply sharing his talent, of making people like his mother smile and think and believe, had once been totally fulfilling. But he'd con- fused that feeling with a racing desire to be anything but himself, to lose his sadness by becoming some- one else. It had led to purposeless craving, a hunger to snag the next commercial, sitcom appearance, or lead role, but it never felt like enough.

When Marlowe had watched the horse step to cen- ter stage earlier that night, he had seen a familiar light in the little horse's eyes that he himself had almost forgotten. In the proud stance of the horse, in the bright call of his whinny, Marlowe saw a creature fulfilled by purpose. He remembered himself as an eight-year-old. Marlowe was sure that Billy could help him get that joy back.

To do that, he had a lot to figure out. First, how to get that horse to Hollywood? He asked the flight attendant for a pen and a motion sickness bag. He placed the paper bag on his knee and began to furiously write on it. Over the next six hours, as the plane flew over Pennsylvania, Ohio, Indiana, Illinois, Missouri, Kansas, Colorado, Utah, and Nevada before finally landing in Los Angeles, California, Marlowe did not stop writing. Marlowe covered every barf bag in the plane. When he'd used them all up, the flight attendant gave him napkins and paper towels. It had started as a loose plan. By the time the wheels of the plane deployed, it was something different entirely. Just before he folded his tray table up for landing, Marlowe finished writing six final words at the top of the very first page:

ONCE UPON A HORSE: THE MOVIE

The rubber of the Cessna's wheels hit the tarmac. Fred woke with a little bit of a snort and wiped some sleepy drool from his chin. He dipped over to the dog bed by his feet and did the same for snoozy Blue. He unclipped his seat belt and unlatched a collapsible wheelchair from where it had been secured to the plane wall. He turned to see his son still seatbelted and holding out a stack of what looked like trash. As Fred took in the words written over every inch of it—it was a screenplay!—a wide smile crept across his face.

"Astonishing!" Marlowe's father said.

Chapter 5

THE PHONE CALL

"Lori, honey, I have to talk to you about something." Her mother's soft voice barely crept past the barn door over which she spoke. A hint of worry wavered through Tessa's tone, and that little wobble in her voice was so unusual for the confident, horse truck–driving lawyer who was her mother that Lori responded as if her mother had shouted.

Lori was in the horse stall picking out Billy's foot, holding the hard keratin of its surface firmly in her hand while she dug out pebbles from around his frog. Her hands were stained purple, but not from art class earlier in the day. She had been squirting antiseptic into the crevices beside the horse's toe that could get damp and soggy—and breed bacteria. To protect Billy from a type of infection called thrush, Lori was dripping bright purple liquid in the grooves. If thrush spread, it could cause him hoof pain, or what's known as lameness, and Lori was diligent at preventing that. Horses, unlike humans, can't really do bed rest if they are injured. They have to keep moving, eating, and digesting constantly to stay healthy. *We* can lay in bed and loaf around to get well; a horse who does that will get sicker. "No hoof, no horse," the veterinarian had said in a singsong voice on a recent visit, teaching her how to apply the violet medicine. But it was a deeply important saying that applied to more than just equines: If you neglect the details, it meant you put all the rest at risk.

Hearing her mother's whispered shout, Lori dropped the cap of the thrush medicine in the shavings in the stall. Letting go of Billy's hoof, she fished out the cap and absentmindedly wiped her lilac fingertips on her jeans. Billy bobbed her with his nose. He'd stood so quietly for the hoof medicine—surely that meant apples? *Not now, Billy*, she told him with her eyes. Something important was happening, Lori was sure. Horses are herd animals, and that means they are extraordinarily sensitive. They hear the slightest rustle in the bushes, even the faraway crunch of a leaf. They can feel a heart beat faster and sense when breathing grows rapid, even before humans realize what is happening. It's a safety mechanism for these big, gentle creatures. The only way for them to stay safe in the wild is to stay very aware. That way, if a leaf in the forest goes "crunch" under the paw pads of a wolf, a horse is already galloping away. In this way, Lori was a lot like a horse on the inside. Growing up in the stalls and spending time in tune with the creatures, Lori had developed that same sensitivity. It helped her navigate the world with empathy, but sometimes it got in the way when she was so concerned about how others felt that she didn't stop to think about how things made *her* feel. Right then, she knew the way a horse did of danger in the distance, just by the notes hiding in her mother's voice.

"Mama," she said, coming up to the half door and resting her elbows over it. "What's wrong?"

In the late-afternoon light, her mother's words caught in her throat. For a long time, Tessa had tried to stay strong for Lori, to not burden her daughter with just how hard she worked to hold on to the farm—and how it was now nearly impossible. But at that moment the pressure welled up, and a small sob escaped her throat. Tessa was afraid she had just done something very, very wrong.

She'd taken a call earlier that day at the law office that had seemed friendly enough. "Ma'am, my name is Fred Narang, and I'm a Hollywood agent, and typically when I make these calls, I say something like, 'I'm gonna make you a star,'" the man had said. Ms. Allegria sat back in her desk chair, wondering where the heck this odd conversation was going. "But today I'm going off script. Never done *this* before." He cleared his throat. Ms. Allegria put her heels on her desk, amused now and more than a little curious. "I'll start again: Ma'am, my name is Fred Narang and . . . I'm gonna make your *horse* a star."

Out across the phone line from Los Angeles unspooled the story of Marlowe's film idea. (Marlowe himself needed no introduction, of course; there probably wasn't a person in America unfamiliar with the Kibble Kid.) Lori's mom listened, nodded, and wondered, *Why on earth is this man, Fred, calling me?!* Until he got to the end. "Marlowe's movie idea, *Once Upon a Horse*, has sold to Ithilien Pictures Productions—it's a major production company. They're making the kid's film!" Fred said over the phone with obvious glee. "Written by *and* starring the planet's biggest child star—the story just makes its own headlines, doesn't it, Ms. Allegria?" And then the reason for the phone call: "My son, Marlowe, wants your horse to be his costar."

There in the stall, Lori listened to her mother's story about the strange phone call. She noticed with her soft, horselike sensitivity, how her mother was telling her what should have been a fun story with a hitch in her voice, with eyes that seemed to shine with tears. As Tessa spoke to her daughter, Lori unconsciously slid her purple-stained fingers up her Fjord horse's neck, until they tangled in his mane and mingled with his jet-black dorsal stripe. A faint smear of violet dragged across his crest, but the girl and the horse didn't mind. They leaned toward each other unconsciously, reacting to her mother's rising heart rate, the tightness in her chest. They sensed something was wrong. It felt like there was a wolf in the woods: Her mother's story wasn't over.

With a gesture of her hand, Lori cut her mother off. Whatever had happened on that phone call, she could see in her mother's eyes that she was hurting. And Lori knew that her mother would never hurt her daughter if she could help it. If she had something painful to reveal, it was because she had no other choice.

"Mama, whatever happened on that call," Lori said, her other hand trembling slightly on the soft yellow neck of her beloved friend, "I understand."

Tessa reached over the Dutch door and clasped her daughter to her chest, ignoring the splintery wood between them. "Lori, I'm so sorry, honey. He offered me enough money to save the farm." Both of them were crying now. Lori knew the next words before her mother even spoke them. And somehow, so did the little Fjord horse beside her.

"Billy is leaving for Hollywood."

Chapter 6

GOODBYE

The horse truck grumbled to life, and inside Billy repositioned his hooves for balance. A little breeze ruffled his stripy mane through the small sliding windows in the trailer's side, and he stood on the tips of his hooves to get his eyes over the sill and peer out at the Springs farm receding behind them. The taste of Granny Smiths was still on his tongue, along with something else: the damp salt on Lori's face when moments before he snuffled her goodbye.

The Fjord horse knew this goodbye was different than others. In past adventures in the horse truck, he'd been sent off with fizzy excitement from his young friend, with pats and scritches and promises to see him at his destination. They were always fun. He particularly loved it when the truck brought him to a competition called a hunter pace, where he and Lori would career through the woods, jumping little logs and splashing through streams. Today Lori had flung her arms around him and shivered and bit her lip, doing her best not to cry. She knew that Billy, her friend who made her feel confident when school brought her down, who helped her with her vocab quizzes and book reports just by being there and never judging, was giving her family yet another gift—the gift of keeping a roof over their heads and the Springs farm their own. She soothed herself by thinking of the obvious joy the little horse got from performing. She thought of him on the stage, of his puffed-out chest, his proudly arching neck, his ears swiveling to catch every last drop of applause. That would be his life now.

She didn't know when she'd see him again. On that phone call, Tessa and Fred had arranged for a lease for the duration of filming *Once Upon a Horse*. But Lori knew from her mother that Fred had angled hard for Billy to be sold outright. The two grown-ups had ended up talking for hours, about the horse, then about their children, and then about their lives. Fred shared that he hadn't seen the light in his son's face like when Marlowe spoke of Billy since forever . . . not since his mother was well and tapping across their old shop floor in new Mary Janes.

"I use a wheelchair, but I actually grew up a horse kid, riding at a therapeutic equestrian center in Queens in New York," Fred told Tessa that night. "Those horses lent me their legs; they shared their joy—my pony was named Joy, in fact!" he said. "I think my kid needs some of that joy right now." He offered her an extraordinary sum of money for Billy. Tessa went so silent Fred thought she had hung up. Ambivalence filled the quiet. But on the other end of the line, she was shaking her head no.

"I can't do it to her," Tessa said, clutching the receiver.

They kept talking. Tessa found herself confiding that over the past year, it was Billy alone to whom her silent daughter spoke. Though they could desperately use the money, Lori needed the Fjord horse more. Fred understood. They agreed to work out a contract for a lot less money. Billy would be leased to Ithilien Pictures Productions just for the filming, however long it took (and if *Once Upon a Horse* was a box-office smash, maybe a few sequels too). After a long discussion, they had agreed to a deal.

But then they didn't hang up. The two parents shared their fears and hopes for their two very different children. Over the phone line from Los Angeles to Springs on the other side of the country, Tessa and Fred spoke long into the night.

And now it was the morning of the Fjord horse's departure. The light slanted through the barn door as mother and daughter stood in Billy's stall. Together they pulled a halter, a head-collar for horses, cushioned with sheepskin, over Billy's ears, which would protect him for the journey. Lori put on her strongest face for her mother. Tessa had deep circles under her eyes, not just from her sadness over sending Billy across the country, but because she'd been working overtime, spending endless nights at the law office. She had to. On a wind-whipped autumn night a few weeks prior, the roof of the barn had partially ripped off, exposing Elaine's stall and the feed room beside it to the elements. It was a miracle the thoroughbred was unscathed, just sopping wet in her roofless stall when they arrived in the morning to a scene of destruction. That included a season's worth of stored sweet feed soaked and inedible. In a way it was a lucky disaster: Exposed, the old timber beams underneath were revealed to be rotted to the core. They could have collapsed on the horses! Every last beam had to be replaced. By the day of his departure, the storm had already gobbled up Billy's equine acting money, and then some.

"Mom," Lori said as she snapped the throatlatch of the halter closed under Billy's yellow jowl. A tarp over the hole in the barn ceiling cast a blue light on their faces. "I know you only leased Billy. But if what you really need is to sell him"—she took a ragged breath—"I understand." Her mother grabbed her hand over the little horse's mane and held it tightly in hers. The black and gold threads braided around their clasped fingers.

"There is no one like you, Lori Allegria," her mother said. "I know it, Billy knows it. I just hope you know it too."

When Billy strode up the ramp of the trailer later that morning, he felt something was different. He knew from his girl's eyes and the salt he tasted when he snuffled her cheek that he was not on his way to a joyful hunter pace or even to Lincoln Center. Yet the horse was unaware of the truth in her tears.

Billy did not know that Tessa had called Fred back the morning he was to leave, with her daughter's permission. Billy did not know he had been sold.

The road was 2,672 miles long to his destination: the Mojave Desert. Not far from Las Vegas, in Nevada, the dusty red range was where *Once Upon a Horse* was shooting its first scenes. Marlowe had dreamed up a western-themed film. He played the son of an outlaw who'd been arrested by a corrupt sheriff. It was up to Marlowe's character to mete out cowboy justice—all on the back of his trusty black-and-yellow horse. But to get that horse there would take a thirty-nine-hour drive! And Billy would stand the whole way in a box stall. But it was a carefully planned road trip: every ten or so hours, there was an overnight stay, not at a hotel, but at various stables along the way booked in advance. For the long and arduous journey, Marlowe had hired a veteran groom and shipper named Julian Okwonga.

It was fall that morning in Springs when Julian's truck grumbled away, Billy jouncing, his legs akimbo for balance, munching hay stuffed in a hanging net. As the hours and days wore on, the horse felt something change. The crisp autumn air of his hometown gave way to softer smells, to breezes through the little window that felt strangely like summer, perplexing him: Winter should have been coming next, right? And shouldn't Lori be coming along? She hadn't climbed into the truck cab beside the driver, Julian. Where *was* she?

He let out a shrill little whinny of worry.

They pulled over at a rest stop. Julian walked around the trailer to reach through the small window and tousle his forelock. He murmured a few lines of poetry to Billy. The horse could not understand, of course, but he understood gentleness, and his tummy relaxed a little. Julian's gentle way reminded the horse of Lori, of her soft hands and kind voice and how she'd practice flash cards or read him her book reports, sitting cross-legged in the shavings in the little nook below where the manger was nailed to the wall. He missed just simply being with her, enjoying their herd of two.

As they rumbled on, the Fjord horse craned his tufted head and smokey black ears to catch what he could out the slit of his window. Highway had slipped by for days, lined with cities and homes and smokestacks and strip malls. Now the view he glimpsed was a red expanse, puckered by strange shapes in orange, rust, and rose. The air was hot. The grand mesas of the Mojave, flat-topped mountains, towered like the facade of Lincoln Center over the landscape. Their sandstone flanks were golden in the late-afternoon light as the horse peered out with wonderment—then he settled. The color reminded him of the curtains of the Metropolitan Opera, the most joyful place he'd ever set hoof.

And so, when the truck finally rolled to its last stop at the Mojave National Preserve, Billy's demeanor had brightened. That same tingling pull that had drawn him to center stage had somehow put Lori in the back of his mind. He felt *excited*—though a little sore from standing so long and very ready for a nice scratchy roll in some good, clean dirt. The twenty million acres of the Mojave Desert sprawled across three states—Nevada, California, and Arizona—and the sand-spiced air filled the horse's nostrils with unfamiliar smells as he strode down the ramp behind Julian. He scented the sap of gnarled Joshua trees, the funk of bighorn sheep somewhere in the distance—and spooked a little at the slap-slap of a jackrabbit's big back paws scooting through the dust.

He tipped up his blond chin. The spires of the Castle Mountains jutted into the horizon. But below them, in the barren landscape, people were *everywhere*.

It was a ghost town, a once prosperous place that had fallen into disrepair long before. Nearly two centuries earlier, pioneers had built this place in the desert, amid the cacti and the mountain lions slinking among them. They came in the 1850s, digging into the mountainsides for silver, gold, copper, and zinc. Fuzzy burros with long ears imported all the way from Africa worked at their sides, trotting down into the mines and hauling the minerals out in packs on their backs. The sweat of the donkeys and the pioneers built the dazzling new metropolis nearby: Las Vegas.

There was a dry goods store, the old sheriff's headquarters, and a five-and-dime. They lined a slim, unpaved road that had once been full of swishing skirts and boots with spurs that jangled off the heels. But after a century of mining, most of the minerals, the iron and the tungsten that powered a hot new invention in 1879—the lightbulb!—had been scraped from the rock. When there was nothing left to mine, the miners fled this tough town and others like it for softer lives in the city of Vegas they had helped set aglow.

The town was abandoned. Unemployed, the burros were turned loose in the desert and galloped away.

The little horse planted his feet at the end of Julian's lead rope and stared at the battered remains of the town: the slumping roofs, the rotting clapboard, the empty spaces where windows had long ago shattered. His ears pricked forward down Main Street. Because this abandoned town was anything but. The ghost town was *alive* with people.

Wearing all black, people ran to and fro across the landscape, clipboards in hands, headsets on ears. A crane called a jib overarched the whole scene, a camera mounted on the end of a long pole called a boom. A camera operator sat in the crane's control room, or cab, panning her lens across the horizon. The sun was just beginning to dip toward the Castle Mountains, but four huge spotlights called klieg lights were lit up like torches. Their beams washed everything in morning-bright light, from the film cameras on tripods positioned around the scene to the canvas director's chairs just behind them. In the glow, more people, some in swinging hoopskirts or swashbuckling leather chaps, struck poses. They burst through the swinging saloon doors over and over or jangled spurs as they strutted down Main Street. The people in black flitted about the costumed characters, adjusting their positions a little bit and scribbling notes.

It was a giant rehearsal. The ghost town had been transformed into a movie set.

"Welcome to the world of *Once Upon a Horse*, Mr. Okwonga! Thank you for delivering our star!" said a voice to their left. The horse turned his muzzle to the sound. A man in a wheelchair scooted through the dust, his hand extended to shake Julian's. A big black Lab trotted beside him. She had a red-and-white paisley bandana around her neck, her tongue lolling in the heat. It was Fred Narang and Blue. The men exchanged greetings and Billy's lead rope. Billy's temporary home would be a wooden stall under a blue-and-white tent set up "backstage"—really the backside of the ghost town's crumbly buildings. Julian Okwonga took a bottle of water gratefully from Fred and tousled Billy's forelock one more time. Then he climbed back in his cab and began his long journey back east with a rumble and a wave.

Fred Narang was an old salt of a horseman. When he was a young boy, his parents had taken him for therapeutic riding lessons and hippotherapy. (That's a type of therapy that involves horses to improve things like motor skills, to name a few. *Hippos* is the Greek word for horse!) Horses are wonderful healers, whether they are needed for a troubled soul or a troubled body. Fred had been born with a condition called cerebral palsy, which clamped his muscles tight and made it difficult to use his legs.

In school or on the street, he buzzed his electric wheelchair with the skill of a Formula 1 driver. But it was Joy, the therapy pony at the equestrian center near where he grew up in Queens, New York, that first gifted Fred the feeling of freedom. Horses are so generous: they give us their power. When humans sit on their backs, they loan us their grace and their strength. At the riding center, called GallopNYC, on his own, on his pony, Fred could *walk*. Just like everyone else. Even better, in the saddle, he was *taller* than his classmates, even his parents. In lessons, no one looked down on him, quite literally, as they had to when he sat in his wheelchair. They looked him in the eyes—or even looked up to him.

He was so enthralled that he barely noticed what riding Joy was doing for him. Joy, like all horses, was a physical therapist, in a sense: The rocking motion of the pony's trot strengthened his core muscles as he kept his balance astride her. When he pressed his legs to her flanks to ask her to walk on and drove his heels down in his stirrups, he stretched his tight hamstrings and flexed his limbs. Gripping the reins and steering his mount helped him hold pencils at school. Joy helped young Fred control a body that sometimes didn't cooperate. All he cared about was that they were together.

Each summer during college, Fred returned to GallopNYC as a volunteer. He took a course to become certified as a therapeutic riding instructor there, teaching riding lessons to other kids just like him. Reluctantly, he left horses behind for Hollywood, and then further still when he moved to Bullhead City and opened the shoe shop with Fatima. But as a young couple, they had often sat behind the register, doodling plans for a future therapy stable on the backs of empty shoebox lids. "My love, you are all my dreams come true," Fatima liked to say. "One day we'll make this dream happen too." But without her, back in the Hollywood grind, Fred put aside his own passions. He had dedicated his life to filling the hole Fatima had left in their son's life, to making Marlowe's dreams reality. He put his own on hold. Perhaps forever.

When Fred took Billy's lead, the Fjord horse felt calm. Horses have an innate ability to recognize a horseperson. Even a horseperson who has never touched a horse—yep, that's a thing. A horseperson can be anyone, even if they've never petted the fuzzy snoot of a single equine. The only thing that is required is love, and a particular softness—that quiet, generous way of being that horses ask of us. That counts to a horse: They know instantly that such a person is part of their herd. As startling as the whole wild world unfolding in the desert was for the Fjord horse, Billy could tell immediately that Fred was a horseperson. His steady hands and friendly voice brought the stocky yellow horse back to earth.

In the wild, horses follow one another everywhere. Their favorite view is, believe it or not, their herdmate's rump! That is because following the leader makes a horse feel certain, even brave, because they know that they are going in the right direction—the herd always gallops toward safety. Tug on a lead rope and stare at a horse facing them, and you'll most likely get a horse who won't budge. It makes sense if you think like a horse: Horses only look head-on at each other in confrontation; eye to eye is the horsey equivalent of bumping chests and shaking fists. Wouldn't you stop if someone was confronting you? But following one another's swishing tails, they step lively, easy and secure.

Fred pivoted to face away from the Fjord horse with a spin of his motorized wheelchair, holding Billy's lead rope firmly in his right hand. The little horse took a breath. He hadn't seen such a device before, but kind hands and a steady way were familiar and soothing after his long journey. When Fred pushed his joystick forward, Billy dutifully trailed the little puffs of dust from the rubber wheels and Blue's wagging tail.

The sun began to slant and redden. As the trio walked down the main street of the set, there was a delicious vibration in the desert air. The actors, the stunt doubles, the camera operators, the film crew, all felt it. And Billy too. To the little horse, it felt like Lincoln Center all over again. He could almost hear the applause already.

Suddenly the saloon's double doors swung open with a mighty clatter and creak. The whole crew stopped what they were doing and looked up at the commotion. Marlowe, covered in stage makeup, came sprinting down the main street! What looked like bruises on his forehead was livid purple paint. Dark colors painted under his eyes gave him a shadowy, desperate look—perfect for the justice-seeking son of an outlaw he was playing. Yet he glowed with joy.

On set, on *his* set—an unheard-of achievement for a kid of twelve—there were crew members in the hundreds. There were scores of castmates and stunt doubles and extras and makeup and hair artists and costumers and caterers and camera operators and even a set designer to paint the cacti a greener shade of green! Yet even surrounded by people bent on making this silver-screen dream real, Marlowe had been lonely. His life was surrounded by colleagues, not classmates. He hadn't had those since elementary school in Bullhead City. Kids who met him never asked him to go bike riding or to play video games; they wanted his autograph. He didn't have pals; he had fans. As he raced through the set to meet his costar, he was overcome with the feeling that in Billy he'd at last find what he wanted even more than an adorable Fjord horse: a friend.

"My horse! The star horse!" he squealed. A group of extras chuckled as they watched the actor sprint by. Clutching a script, the director raced after Marlowe out of the saloon, pleading with him to get back to rehearsal. Marlowe barreled down the street and—hi-yah!—leapt over a tumbleweed that had drifted on set. In seconds he was at Billy's side, beads of sweat sticking his hair to his forehead. When he reached the Fjord horse, he flung his arms around the crest of his neck. "Billy! I'm so happy you're here!"

It was *not* the way you should greet a horse. Especially not a horse who just completed a nearly three-thousand-mile journey to a wholly unknown place with wholly unknown people. Luckily Billy was used to enthusiasm from Lori. Like the time she barged squealing into his stall with the "most improved" certificate she'd earned in geometry after they'd drilled hypotenuse and isosceles while prancing through a hunter pace. And so, he leaned into Marlowe's bear hug and his joy. Then the horse's tummy knotted a bit. With all the newness, all the change, there in Marlowe's arms was the first time he had let himself think of Lori. This boy was kind. But the other member of Billy's herd was missing. It hurt.

"Been a while since we've seen our Marlowe this enthusiastic, eh, girl?" Fred said to Blue, after the hugs were exchanged and Billy once again tailed the man on the way to his tented stall. The director wrangled Marlowe back into rehearsal. As they walked through the set, the black Lab on one side of his wheelchair, the Fjord horse strolling alertly on the other, they could hear Marlowe rehearsing his lines. The words slipped over the swinging doors of the saloon stage. "Just you wait, Sheriff. I'll find my father! If only I had a way to cross this desert. If only I had a horse . . ." The young actor's voice was crisp and clear and full of the gusto you'd expect in the anguished son he was playing.

The Kibble Kid was back.

Chapter 7

YOWL!

[Act III; Scene 26 Once Upon a
Horse: The kid cowboy sees a
yellow-and-black horse hidden in
sagebrush. The animal is tangled
in the bushes by his reins. The
kid cowboy takes out a pocket-
knife and cuts the horse free.
The horse, whom no one could
ever tame, is so grateful to the
kid cowboy he lets him mount up.
The sun rises. They gallop off
to seek his father. And justice.]

Safe in his tent stall, Billy had a good, scratchy roll in the shavings. He nibbled at the hay, drank some cool water, and peered between the slats. Outside, the crew was setting the scene for the next day. His movie acting debut! It was the scene in which the kid cowboy finds his dreamed-for horse. Billy would play a runaway gelding that had become trapped by reins tangled in sagebrush. Marlowe would cut him free.

The sagebrush had been prepped. Some of its leaves were even painted with an extra coat of green by the set designer so they would "pop" on-screen! The director had spent the afternoon blocking, or mapping out the positions both horse and boy would take. As the sun sank low over the Castle Mountains, a costumer visited the cozy stall and fit Billy for a western bridle. It was different from the English bridle he wore with Lori, which wrapped snugly around his face with a slim bit. This bridle hung over just one ear, and the bit was unfamiliar. A long metal shank hung outside his lip. He tumbled it for a few moments in his mouth until it sat comfily in the groove behind the last of his forty teeth. When it was perfectly adjusted, the costumer took it off, fed him a carrot, and wished the horse good night.

As the crew filed out, a production assistant came by with a big bucket of *delicious* bran mash. A motorcade of four-wheelers and trucks headed off into the darkening desert. The set was quiet as the sun hid behind the Castle Mountains. Billy slurped his dinner. A desert orchestra began to play: Instead of the Lincoln Center drums and violins, flutes and harps, trumpets and trombones, a chorus of Jerusalem crickets scritched from their burrows in the sand dunes. Kelso shieldbacks buzzed their own symphony. In his stall, his belly full, the little yellow horse huffed a sleepy sigh.

Horses doze mostly, standing on all four feet. Alert to danger, they rest most often this way. But it is not true that they do not lie down to sleep. For about one or two hours a day, they curl their legs beneath them or stretch out on their sides and fall into deep slumber. Sometimes their ears twitch and their tail flicks, and you can tell they are dreaming. But no one shall ever know about what. Weary beyond all measure, Billy sank into his soft bed. He tucked his fetlocks and hocks—his ankles—beneath his bulky body, till he was curled up like a kitten. His chin dropped to the straw. Billy was too tired to dream. The next day the horse would become an actor! But first: sleep.

YOWL.

A noise! A brutal, beastly growl. Billy whipped himself to his hooves, scrabbling to stand in the straw. Every hair vibrated. It was a violent, predatory noise. The call of a barn cat mixed with the snarl of a bear. All around was the kind of dark only a desert got: total. The klieg lights were long shut off. The generators that powered the movie set were cut for the night. A guard snoozed in a pickup truck nearby. Everywhere was velvety blackness—the exact opposite of the glow of Lincoln Center—except for pinpricks of stars that blanketed everything above. He held his breath.

YOWL!

Billy's cinder-tipped ears shot forward. He was instantly not just wide awake but armed: without thinking, his haunches, or hindquarters, bunched in readiness for a kick. The tent stall had seemed so cozy and safe seconds earlier; now the little horse realized the blue-and-white fabric over it was no protection at all. *What was that noise?!*

Horses have some of the largest eyes of any mammal on land, and those outsized eyes are perfectly adapted for the dark. Inside our eyes, and theirs, are specially shaped receptors that let in color and light. The ones that take in the light, those are called rods. The parts of eyes that see color are cones. Horses have a lot more rods than cones, which means they have terrific vision in dimness. So while they may not see as many colors as we do, in the darkness they see almost as clearly as owls.

Billy could see outside his flimsy stall into the dark. Right into the reflective eyes of a Mojave mountain lion.

Chapter 8

THE NEWS

Two thousand six hundred and seventy-two miles away, Lori spent the hours of Billy's journey scouring headlines on her computer. She was looking for news of Marlowe's splashy movie production—and her tubby little horse's arrival. Marlowe was constantly making headlines. "'Kibble Kid' Buys Star Horse," one read, detailing all about how Marlowe had purchased Billy practically off the stage at Lincoln Center. "From Child Star to Preteen Producer?" read another. That article was a breathless account from a reporter who had visited the ghost town set in the Mojave where filming was taking place. (Fred Narang had been right; it was such an unusual event that the headlines practically wrote themselves!)

Tessa watched and worried as her daughter shuffled through her barn chores each morning in the days after her horse departed. Lori used to start her days skipping with a blueberry muffin in hand to Billy's stall. The boarding horses, BonBon and Express Lane, were gentle and understanding, as all horses are when we are down and out. Yet they were simply not her Billy. But Lori really tried to keep her chin up. The barn roof was nearly repaired, and the splintering timber was in the process of being painstakingly replaced. Tessa had put the leftover money (and there was a lot of it— Fred had been exceptionally generous) into Lori's college fund. When she heard that, Lori was even more grateful for Billy; the special little horse had given her love since the time she was born. Now he was helping provide for her future. But she missed him. So much.

On the fifth day after Billy's departure, Lori and her mother got a text from Julian Okwonga. It was one of his signature poems:

Billy the Fjord horse traveled far

On his way to be a star

Don't be sad, don't you fret

He's arrived safe on the movie set!

It was cute, yet Lori's chin trembled a little. But thinking of her horse being in good hands helped.

Then the next morning before school, she turned on the television. There was a picture of Billy on the screen. The chyron read: MISSING.

Lori screamed in the living room, but her mother had left for the office at daybreak, so there was no one to come running. The news anchor's words sizzled through the girl, paralyzing her in front of the screen.

"Terrible news on set at a new production filming in the Mojave Desert not far from Las Vegas," the anchor intoned. "The buzzy Kibble Kid movie, *Once Upon a Horse*, was set to start shooting its main scenes today, after the long-awaited arrival of Marlowe Narang's unusual costar, a Norwegian Fjord horse named Bobby," she said.

"It's Billy," Lori said out loud to no one, her voice cracking. She had slid off the couch. She would be late for school, but she didn't care. Now she was on her knees on the carpet, her face almost against the TV screen. "But overnight, hours after the horse arrived all the way from the East Coast, he broke loose from the set and vanished. According to a spokesman for the production, signs point to a possible mountain lion attack." In her living room, Lori felt faint. The clip flashed to a dusty western set. In front of a news camera, with dozens of microphones pointed at his mouth, was a man. The name "Fred Narang" ticked across the screen.

"Billy is alive; he has to be," Fred said to the reporters. Lori could see his right hand tightly gripping the neck scruff of the big black Lab beside him, as if for security. "We believe that the horse fought off a mountain lion attack sometime overnight, and in doing so kicked down his tent stall. This desert is nearly thirty-one thousand square miles. He could be anywhere out there by now—but we are not giving up on him," Fred said.

In the background of the shot, Lori thought she could make out a kid in a cowboy hat, slumped on the steps of a derelict five-and-dime, his head in his hands. It had to be Marlowe. Fred looked straight at the camera: "We are calling upon the public to join us in the manhunt—er, horse hunt. We need your help to fan out and find him. Before that mountain lion does again."

Sometimes in a crisis, we collapse, freeze up, break down. That is OK. It is not always the most productive response, not always the best solution for a problem, but if turning inside for a moment steadies you when things are bad, then that is what you need to do, for you. Horses hardly ever react this way, however. When things are dangerous, they *run*. This is *not* because they are cowardly! Anyone who has watched a racehorse career down a track and fight with each powerful stride to win a race for their rider or seen a show jumping horse leap painted poles higher than the tips of their ears knows horses are brave, bold creatures. And smart—at a run is when they can use their most powerful weapon: a good kick at anything in their wake! But they are prey, which means that once, long ago, when they lived in the wild, they had to keep fast steps ahead of creatures who were out to eat them. That impulse has been passed down through all horses. It sticks in their cells, even though now almost all horses live safe from predators in comfy stalls and cozy barnyards. When horses gallop away, they are being a different type of brave.

Lori knelt, breathless, before the TV screen as the news of her horse's disappearance flooded over her. She did not know the details of the encounter with the mountain lion, but she knew that Billy must have been in true danger to flee from humans. They were the thing he adored the most, even more than Granny Smith slices. She snapped to action. In a single motion, Lori grabbed her hoodie and scooped up her backpack, which was waiting by the front door. From between textbooks and notebooks and horse books, she pulled out one of her vocabulary flash cards and a pen and hastily scrawled on the back. She dropped the note on the kitchen table and swiped a green apple from a bowl resting there.

Then she bolted out the front door.

Chapter 9

DONKEYS

Hours earlier and thousands of miles to the west, the mountain lion snuck up to Billy's stall on padded paws. She crept around it twice, surveying the scene, her soft tail lashing. She scented the air, wondering if the Fjord horse would make a good snack for her and her hungry cubs. There in the thick night, Billy watched her with his big, light-collecting eyes. He breathed only a few shallow breaths. Hardly a hair on his dun hide stirred.

There were barn cats in Springs, like a big calico named Skipper who perched on a manger sometimes and headbutted Billy with rumbly purrs as he ate his oats. Occasionally in the fall, a red fox would run through, yipping at her kits to follow. A parade of raccoons and possums regularly threw all-night dance parties if Lori forgot to secure the lid on the garbage bin behind the barn. Those animals ate meat, yes, but they were no threat to Billy. They had never set his fur on edge. Billy was now operating on instinct. Generations of prey-creature knowledge were braided into his very being. He had never seen a mountain lion, but he knew the prowler's presence meant danger.

And so, the horse ran. Right into the wall of his makeshift stall, bashing it with his thick shoulder and broad forehead. And then he kicked! Each of his saucer feet, which Lori had so carefully made sure were in tiptop condition, landed with precision on the back wall behind him.

Bang! Bang! BANG!

He plunged and bucked, his hooves hitting home again and again on the stall wall. All at once, his furious striking, heaving, and kicking did what he had hoped: he brought the blue-and-white-striped tent crashing down. The vinyl tent roof landed right on his head. Billy shook out his blond forelock, dazed and disoriented for a minute. Then he shook like a retriever shook water from their coat, and in a few more moments he was untangled from the heap of plywood and bunting that had confined him. He was free!

And face-to-face with the mountain lion.

On the stage at Lincoln Center, Billy had played a warrior horse. Now, thousands of miles away, he needed to be a warrior again. This time for real. The cat slid forward, her long claws unsheathed. They made no sound in the desert dust. The small horse drew breath. He puffed up his chest. He raised his muzzle:

WHINNY!

For a split second, the lioness was stunned. Billy seized the moment. He bolted away into the night.

Hours later, Billy knew the mountain lion was far behind him; his sweaty flank and the foam on his thick neck made sure that was true. He had galloped faster than any hunter pace with Lori, and then galloped faster still. His hooves clattered across loose stone, or scree, and then sank into sand. Sagebrush clawed at his pasterns, or ankles, and the thorns of silver cholla cacti clung to his tail. But still he galloped on, until he was sure that those claws and the lioness they belonged to were lost in his trail of desert dust. When he finally slowed to a canter, and then, spent, to a trot, he became rapidly aware that his hoofbeats were not the only ones out there.

Billy was not alone in the desert.

Dawn broke over the Castle Mountains, and rusty red light slipped across its four summits, revealing the strangest horses he had ever seen. He swiveled his wedge head. Long-eared and smoke colored, with sooty tips and inky dorsal stripes like Billy, the odd horselike-but-not-quite creatures surrounded him on all sides. They looked at him alertly with eyes like jet-colored beads. He knew they were friendly because they were smiling as equines do— not with their lips like us humans, but with their ears. If the creatures' ears had been pressed flat against their skulls, he might have been worried: That is a horse's version of a scowl. But a dozen pairs of ears were pricked toward him; their ears were smiling. Lazily, some whipped their tails at their flanks, swatting bothersome bloodsucking insects called kissing bugs.

Those tails! Billy's chocolate eyes fairly popped out of his skull. Long strands of hair hung from his tail, as did the ones connected to the rumps of every horse he'd ever seen, from Clydesdale to thoroughbred. But these equines had . . . dog tails? They were kind of like the tail that swung from the rump of that Labrador he'd met the day before. Except they each had a little tuft of black hair at the tip. To his right, a big, charcoal-colored male dragged his hoof in the sand. This was a challenge. Billy heard it loud and clear—"I see you, don't come any closer"—in the language of gestures equines share, no matter what they look like. Then the soot-colored creature reared back his head in a greeting that, frankly, flabbergasted the Fjord:

Hee-HAW!

There in the first light of morning, Billy had found himself surrounded by a herd of wild donkeys.

Chapter 10

GREYHOUND

For the first time in her entire life, Lori was happy she was so very tall.

Most people, if they saw a twelve-year-old trying to buy a ticket for a Greyhound bus from one side of the continent to the other, all by themselves, would intervene. *"Where are your parents?"* the ticket booth attendant might say. *"Do your caregivers know you are trying to board this bus alone?"* the driver might ask. And adults should ask because it is *not* safe for a child to cross the country without a jot of supervision. What Lori was doing was supremely dangerous, even if she believed it was for a good reason: She was running away.

Yet Lori was taller than the ticket taker, taller than even the bus driver. She pulled her hoodie down around her face and low over her eyes and spoke in as grown-up a voice as she could muster. She forked over almost every dollar she had—over the years, the boarders at the barn had given her little tips for chores like mucking BonBon's stall or currying mud from Elaine after she rolled in the muck. Her hand trembled as she pressed the bills through the slot at the ticket counter.

The busy bus station staff hardly looked up as they handed over her ticket. A few minutes later, up the steps of the bus, the driver punched her ticket without a second glance. They mistook her, as so many others often did, for a grown-up. *It was almost too easy for something so wrong, this running away,* she thought. The bus pulled away from the Springs Bus Depot, and she sunk low into her seat. She pulled the cords of her hood even tighter—to cover her face as well as her shame at doing something so naughty—as it chugged toward the Mojave.

Fifty-eight hours. That was how long Lori was on that bus as it lurched across New Jersey, Pennsylvania, Ohio, Indiana, Illinois, Missouri, Kansas, Colorado, and Utah on its way to the desert. She considered eating Billy's Granny Smith in her backpack, until a kindly old woman in the seat across from her gave her three extra PB&J sandwiches she'd packed for her grandson, who was cuddled beside her. Lori slept curled in a ball, leaning against the window, or read the equine encyclopedia she'd accidentally brought along in her bookbag. She pored over images of wiry Akhal-Tekes from a place called Turkmenistan and Appaloosas from out West, who looked covered in confetti. Whenever the bus stopped for people to stretch their legs, Lori kept her hoodie pulled up and the drawstring tight. She was afraid someone would figure out she was a twelve-year-old off in the world on her own. She was afraid someone would stop her.

That was how long her phone buzzed and buzzed with texts from her mother, asking where she was with increasing desperation. When she left, Lori had not intended to upset her mom; she had just been single-mindedly focused on her belief that her horse needed her. She had not thought of the consequences of her actions on others. Now she felt sick with the fear her mother must be feeling. As her absence stretched into its third day, Lori wrote back. A little. She felt terrible. But she did not want to be stopped.

Just a few miles over the Nevada border was the ghost town set of *Once Upon a Horse* and, she hoped, a little lost Fjord horse waiting to be found. The bus wheezed to a stop. Lori grabbed her knapsack and skedaddled down the steps and onto the dusty street.

Bullhead City, Arizona.

The first thing she saw was *heaven*: There was a small food stand just outside the rickety bus shelter. Lori sprinted to it. "Whatever you make, I'll take two!" she said. A girl about her age was manning the booth, though her head barely came over the plexiglass partition. She almost spit out her chewing gum laughing. "It's called fry bread," she said. Lori tipped her head to the side. She'd never had one. "Think of it as a Navajo taco—you'll love it." The girl scooped beans from a simmering pot onto a fluffy disc and topped it with shredded lettuce, chopped tomato, and a sprinkle of cheese. Then she giggled, gave a sympathetic shrug, and made Lori another. "And the beans, they're my aunt's recipe. I help her after school in exchange for letting me ride her horse."

Lori gasped out loud without meaning to. Here was another horse lover, she was sure, someone who might understand her, and she so badly needed understanding right now. She was so sad and scared for Billy that she became reckless about revealing herself.

"My horse . . . he's lost!" Now she was blubbering, the paper plates of fry bread sagging in each hand. "He's from Springs, in New York. He's, he's . . . a Norwegian Fjord horse . . . and, well, an actor now. There was an opera, and, and . . . and now there's a mountain lion!" Lori broke down. Nothing after that made sense. Her shoulders heaved.

The girl pulled off her apron and ran from behind the plexiglass partition on the booth to Lori's side. "Omigosh. Oh. My. GOSH. Marlowe Narang's horse? I saw that story on the news!" the girl said. When Lori looked up, she saw the girl's face was as stricken as her own. "I've read all about it, and there's even a group online called Pony Tales I'm part of that is tracking his hoofprints across the Mojave and posting his last known location online. Don't cry! Don't cry! They're about to find him, I'm so, so sure. That's the one the papers are calling the 'Star Horse'?"

"M-m-my horse," Lori corrected her. She was weeping again now. "And he's lost."

Chapter 11

APPALOOSA

The girl was tiny compared to the tall stranger, but she wrapped Lori in a huge hug. Lori needed the hug so badly she leaned her chin onto the top of her new friend's head and cried.

"First things first, introductions: I'm Aiyana. And I know how you feel," she said, without taking her arms from around Lori. Though they had never met, neither felt awkward at all. They were horse people, and they instantly understood the heartbreak of losing a member of their herd.

"If I lost my horse Sǫ-Sǫ, I think I'd fall apart," Aiyana said. "Luckily you have the cutest guy in the world out looking for him."

Lori laughed a little at that, even through her sniffles. "I'm Lori," she said into the hug. "You're a *fan*?"

Aiyana pulled back, happy that she'd gotten Lori to smile, and continued. "Oh yeah, I'm a Kibble Kid *super*fan—Marlowe grew up in Bullhead City, you know? But no one really got to know him, 'cause they pulled him out of school back in, like, second grade. I have practically every one of his movies, and I even made my dad wait in line at the Colorado River Nature Center for, like, almost a day. His mom—she died—was, like, a rafting guide, and Marlowe shot a dog food commercial paddling the rapids there with, get this, a black Lab in a kayak!" Aiyana was chatty and smiley, and giggles ran under her words like a skipping creek. "But Dad forgot to bring a movie poster or anything, so I literally got an autographed can of dog food!" They both burst out laughing. Everything was scary for Lori right now. But it was always good to laugh.

Aiyana put her hand on Lori's shoulder and looked up into her wet eyes. "Look, I'm supposed to watch my auntie Tallulah's fry bread booth for another half hour before I have to do my stable chores and then start homework, but this is *clearly* an emergency. A horse emergency." As she slipped around to the back side of the plexiglass, Aiyana hurriedly put covers on the pots of beans and wrapped the shredded cheese in tinfoil. "And we have to do something. Plus, my auntie is the one who got me crazy for barrel racing on Sǫ-Sǫ. Yeah . . . he's technically her horse, but my auntie shares! So if anyone will understand, it's going to be her."

Lori took a bite of the one fry bread in her left hand as Aiyana chatted on, nodding. It was scrumptious. After her first few polite bites, she shoveled it—and the second one in her right hand—into her mouth. It was so good, plus there was an extra nourishment in the fact that a new friend had made it—someone who instantly understood her because they shared a passion: horses.

"What's barrel racing?" Lori asked through her final mouthful.

"Oh. Em. Gee. You have not lived until you've tried it! Sǫ-Sǫ is fully obsessed with it." Aiyana finished packing up the little shop, slipped her arm through Lori's elbow, and started walking. Lori was relieved to not be alone anymore.

"It's a rodeo sport, and there are three barrels in the arena. You gallop like *mad* at them and run a cloverleaf pattern around them. Fastest around them wins big. It is *so* much harder than it looks because if you go too fast, you go wide, and that adds seconds to your time. Too slow, and you're, well, too slow!" She smiled at her own little joke and steered Lori down the street a bit farther. "Sǫ-Sǫ is so good at it because he used to be a ranch horse. He could track cows and spin circles around them to round them up practically on his own." She closed her eyes, and Lori could see she was reliving her most thrilling rides behind her lids. Lori knew because she did that exact same thing after a brilliant hunter pace. "*He's* super good at it, but I kinda struggle. See, So̱-So̱ is better with a little motivation—you know, boot-heel pressure—but I'm so short my legs reach only half-way down his flanks! So I can't get his motor going when we practice at home or on the trails." Lori looked down at Aiyana's short legs scurrying a little to keep pace with her lanky ones. Aiyana tittered. "Auntie says I'll grow into him."

"But in the arena . . . no motivation necessary, So̱-So̱ is a star. He *loves* performing." She shuddered a little at the thrill of her tale. "Lori, with barrels, when you're really flying and really turning and burning—so fast and sharp your horse is almost parallel to the *ground,* and it's like I can't tell where I end and So̱-So̱ begins—there is simply nothing like it in the world." She squeezed Lori's elbow at the joy of it.

"I've felt that way, too, but on a hunter pace!" Lori replied.

Aiyana squinched up her eyes. "A hunter pace?"

"The forest passes by so fast it's like a soft green blur, a feeling more than a place, you know?" Lori said. Aiyana nodded. "And there are obstacles, like logs and stone walls in front of you, but they're not scary or intimidating because your horse, well, my horse, Billy, he just . . . I dunno . . . shares his power."

"Exactly! It's a gift horses give us." Aiyana sighed. "I'm so grateful."

"Me too," Lori agreed.

When Aiyana stopped walking Lori realized she had been so engrossed in their conversation that she hadn't thought to ask where they had been headed. Her new friend gently directed her to turn to her side. A vast pasture stretched behind a wire fence line at the edge of the road.

And hanging over the fence was the velveteen nose of a stunning horse. A polka-dot one.

Sǫ-Sǫ was an Appaloosa. Lori knew this from the breed books she stashed in her bookbag, colorfully illustrated with pictures of horses from Afghanistan to Zimbabwe. She read about them at recess, between class, any time she was trying to avoid eye contact. She knew that the Appaloosa was a type of horse descended from Spanish stock and bred in North America by the Nimíipuu native people in the 1800s. At the time, the tribe (which is also known as the Nez Perce) was nomadic, which meant they frequently moved their homes from place to place. Their smooth-gaited horses bore entire communities across their territory, galloping over areas now known as Oregon, Idaho, Washington, and Montana, and back again.

Hardy and sure-footed, Appaloosas also have spectacularly different coats: Rather than the plain bays, chestnuts, and grays of other breeds, Appaloosa hides are daubed, splotched, spattered, and splashed with white. They can be dark mahogany or rich chestnut with snowcaps of white on their rumps like someone dolloped frosting from above. Some have white hairs that sparkle through reddish coats or black fur. Sometimes the white glimmering through looks almost blue—that's called roaning. Dark parts like knees and elbows on such frosted horses are known as varnish—maybe because it looks like rich paint has slicked their fur. Some horses look like children's art projects, with wild splashes of paint. Many have light eyes and pink skin where the white drips dribbled over their coats. And some, perhaps the most spectacular of all (but what horse, of any color, is not spectacular in its own way, always?) are like Sǫ-Sǫ: a *leopard* Appaloosa.

Sǫ-Sǫ's body was the brightest white, but every few inches was a loud black splotch. Hundreds of them! He bore his kind's name perfectly: He was as spotted as a leopard, from top to tail. Only his muzzle was perfectly pink, with a few black dots at the end of his nose like freckles.

At the edge of the road, Sǫ-Sǫ turned his fine head to regard Lori with first one eye, then the other.

Horses cannot see directly in front of them because their eyes are perched on either side of their head. To feel comfortable with new things, a horse must show its brain what something looks like with each eye, one at a time, to get the full picture. While they can see nearly 360 degrees around them, right in front of their nose is a *total* blind spot! It makes what they do for people—jump for us, gallop for us, carry us with them on adventures—so much more incredible when you consider it. Think of a jumping horse—as they approach a towering fence or even a tiny crossrail, the obstacle disappears! To bound over what they cannot see is a leap of faith, a testament to their trust in their rider. Horses fly blind—for us.

Sọ-Sọ turned to peer at the girl from Springs, first with his right eye, slightly hidden under his shaggy forelock, then with his left one. When the late-afternoon sun caught his gaze, Lori gasped. His eyes gleamed sky blue.

"Wow, I know they call my Billy the Star Horse these days, but Sọ-Sọ has *stars* in his eyes," Lori said in a soft, awed voice.

"Can you believe one blue eye is actually called a 'walleye' with horses? Isn't that the weirdest name for something so gorgeous?" Aiyana responded, reaching up to scritch the Appy's nose.

"Those blue eyes are why Auntie called him Sǫ-Sǫ." She smiled impishly at Lori.

Lori raised an eyebrow, not following. "Doesn't 'So-So' mean something is kind of 'meh?'" Lori asked. But this horse was spectacular!

Aiyana giggled and smiled impishly. "'Sǫ' means 'star' in Navajo, that's my tribe; I'm Native American. I'm learning the language in tribal school, and I'm kinda good. Anyway, he's 'Sǫ-Sǫ,' one star for each of those starry eyes." Aiyana smiled a sly half smile. "But anyone who doesn't speak our language thinks it means he's just 'blah,' and so they never see this superstar coming till he has smoked them at barrels!" The two girls laughed again as Aiyana ruffled Sǫ-Sǫ's long, multicolored forelock.

Lori reached out to touch his pink nose—not with her hand, but by gently extending her own nose toward him. Horses don't greet with shaking hands or a *howyadoin'?* wave, of course; instead, they blow gently into each other's nostrils and inhale the breath of their new acquaintance and exhale their own. They absorb each other's scent, plus tons of mysterious information only horses know but haven't told us—yet. Lori knew the best way to speak to a horse was to do it in their language, *horse*. Sǫ-Sǫ understood her gesture and leaned in to snuffle the girl from Springs. *This is who I am; who are you?* the Appaloosa's breath said. Lori blew back gently into first one nostril, then his other. *This is me, Lori.* She exhaled. I am here for you.

"I have an idea," Aiyana said. She grabbed a halter off a fence post and slipped it over Sǫ-Sǫ's head. As girl and horse started across the pasture toward a four-stall barn on a hill, she beckoned to Lori to follow.

Chapter 12

MUCKING

"Grab a broom," Aiyana said. Lori found one leaning in a corner and without further instruction began sweeping hay and wood shavings from the aisle in the small barn. She knew barn chores when she saw them! "So I usually take Sǫ-Sǫ out on a trail ride to stretch his legs after I finish my homework—sometimes we practice cloverleafs around the cacti, but usually he just walks because, like I said, he doesn't respect my puny legs. But you're super tall!"

Lori cringed, bracing for what Aiyana would say next—she had felt so at ease with this new girl, not at all self-conscious. Was Aiyana going to end up being just another kid who mocked her? Pinpricks of tears started. Then the girl surprised her: "Together, we can use both our strengths," Aiyana continued. "You can keep Sǫ-Sǫ going with your heels, I'll steer him around the cacti . . . and we can go find Billy out in the Mojave!"

"Let's go *right now*!" Lori squeaked, dropping the broom with a clatter.

"Hold yer horses," Aiyana replied. "If I leave these horses unfed and their stalls unpicked, number one, my aunt will come searching to scold me and find out we're gone, and number two . . ."

Lori finished the sentence for her. "We'd never do that to horses." She picked the push broom back up. "Faster with two people!"

As they tidied the barn, Lori thought about what Aiyana had said about riding double: she had never really thought of her height as a strength. She thought of it as her big (emphasis on big) problem. She spent her days wishing for shorter legs so that she would just blend in. When she woke up every morning with the same (or longer) legs, she vowed to find other ways to keep a low profile if she couldn't do so literally. Ever since her growth spurt started a few years ago, she had become almost silent. Her teachers and her mother and the Fjord horse who loved her tried to tell her she had nothing to hide— certainly not herself. But she was so afraid to say the wrong thing, to draw more attention when she already turned heads on picture day, when strangers asked, "Are you *sure* you're in seventh grade?" So she had silenced herself. In fact, this conversation with Aiyana and Sǫ-Sǫ was the most she'd spoken to a kid she didn't know in her life. And it felt . . . wonderful.

Aiyana popped her head over the stall door, inter-rupting her thoughts. "The only thing is . . . I have a vocab test tomorrow. I really have to study." She bit her lip. "See, I'm here in Bullhead City because I was having a real tough time in school. My mom and dad are both in the military," she said, as a whoosh of shavings and horse droppings flew expertly from the stall and into the bucket. Lori was impressed with her aim. "That means you have to move around *a lot*, wherever they are stationed. I hated all the moving. People picked on me because I was always the new girl and, well." She stopped for a moment and leaned on her pitchfork, searching for words. Lori swept the tangles of hay into a waiting shovel and dumped them into the muck bucket too. "I'm not proud of it, but I, I didn't know what to do, and I was so angry about Mom and Dad moving us around all the time, I started fighting back."

Here Lori used her quietness as a strength. She paused her shoveling to look across the barn deeply at her new friend, and as Billy had done for her, she showed she was listening. Lori picked up an orange bar of glycerin saddle soap and a round yellowish sponge. She dipped the sponge in a bucket of water and wrung it out before smoothing it onto the glossy bar. She began to rub it in circles on the tooled leather of a western saddle resting on a saddle tree. She listened to Aiyana as she ran the sponge over the stirrup leathers, the pommel, and the horn in front, which was so different from her slim English saddle at home. She didn't push Aiyana to tell more than she felt comfortable telling, but she made space for her new friend to share—without judgment—just like her Fjord horse once had.

Aiyana had moved on to pick out another stall. In it was a brown-and-white-splotched miniature horse no taller than her hip. A Falabella, just like Lori had read about in her equine encyclopedia. His stall plate read "Guernsey," like the type of spotted cow he resembled.

Aiyana continued: "So Mom and Dad sent me to live with Auntie Tallulah while they're away on their current deployment, and boy, was I mad. Madder than any time I got into a fight in school. Raging, in fact." As she spoke, she trailed her hand over Guernsey's painted rump, making whorls in his fur with her fingers.

"Guernsey here wouldn't let me within ten feet of him when I arrived," she said. "And Sǫ-Sǫ pinned his ears at me and slashed his tail whenever I tried to come close."

Lori nodded. "They were not mad at you, you know, they were scared of whatever was making you so mad," she said. She moved onto a bridle hanging on a curved tack hook, running the sponge over the cheekpieces, the browband, the curb strap. She took a fresh cloth from a hook and dunked it in clean water to wipe down the bit. "Since horses are prey animals, they are very sensitive to, well, I guess you'd call them *vibes*—it's how they stay safe."

"Exactly!" Aiyana responded. She closed the mini horse's stall behind her and carefully latched it. Then she stepped across the aisle and pulled a bareback saddle blanket and extra pads from a shelf near the saddle racks. "Being around them made me realize that being angry wasn't going to change anything. When I really think about it, my parents are trying to do their jobs and the best for me," she said. She pulled a girth from a hook and slung it over her shoulders. "The horses made me realize my hurt was hurting others," she continued. "I wanted to be the type of person horses and people can trust. I am that now." She blushed. Guernsey, the mini horse, stood on the tips of his hooves to get his snoot over the stall door, begging her for treats. She giggled. "Well, I'm *trying* to be."

"I understand," Lori said. "It may have been the wrong decision, but we can all make those sometimes." She thought about horses, how sometimes prey creatures will startle and run from something they are afraid of—and into another type of danger by accident. Galloping away, they can end up tangled in brush, tripping over stones, twisting a fetlock. Horses act on instinct and don't have the tools to make other choices. But humans do. In fact, Aiyana was making different choices now. Lori thought about her own decision to silence her voice, to hide from the world. If she had done that when she got off the bus, she would never be sharing this special moment in the quiet barn with a new friend. *Going forward*, she thought as she finished wiping the bit until it gleamed, *I will make a different decision*.

"Grab a brush; let's groom Ṣǫ-Ṣǫ up," Aiyana said. She pulled two round currycombs, a hoof pick, and two stiff bristle brushes from a crate nailed to the wall at the far end of the barn. The two got to work on the Appaloosa, rubbing the currycombs in circles on either side of his spotty body, loosening the dirt. Lori looked over the ridge of his withers at the other girl.

"Thank you for sharing. You're really brave," Lori said. Aiyana broke into a wide smile.

"Thanks for saying that. But it doesn't change one big problem: If we go out searching now, how am I going to study for my vocabulary test tomorrow?"

Lori clapped the brushes together to clear off the dust. "Billy is amazing at vocab! We practice together all the time," she said. Aiyana burst out laughing, and so did Lori when she realized how what she had said came across. "Ha ha! No, he's a *horse*, *duh*; he doesn't speak English. What I mean is I always practice my vocabulary words beside him in his stall;

it gives me space to think. I can help you practice while we go look for him!" That sold it. Aiyana nodded. She was sure they would not get in trouble if they were doing homework *while* they rode.

Aiyana whipped out her phone and looped a lead-rope over her shoulder. "I'm going to post to the Pony Tales group and tell them we're joining the search party and that we're heading out into the Mojave."

Lori nodded enthusiastically, but then her shoulders fell. There was a whole desert out there—finding a dust-colored horse in miles of sand? Impossible. "There is no way we will find him," Lori said. Aiyana didn't seem to hear her; she was busy unlocking the fence.

"You're right. We will never find him," Aiyana said, slipping the bridle over the Appaloosa's ear and sliding the bit gently into his mouth. She handed Lori a riding helmet and pulled on her own. "If we don't try."

Chapter 13

THE SEARCH

Tessa Allegria arrived on the *Once Upon a Horse* set like a tornado of worry. She hadn't found Lori's note until late after work the night she left, and hadn't slept since: She spent the first frantic days of Lori's absence searching every last corner of Springs with the Springs Police Department. Everyone was unable to fathom at first that this shy, well-behaved child had really set out alone across the continent to find the little lost horse. "She's just bluffing," the police sergeant told Tessa. "Mad you sold her horse off. She'll turn up by supper." When Lori's first text message came, her mother knew it was not a bluff— she jumped on a plane to the desert. Her eyes were hollow and red. She had cried the entire flight. She wasn't angry with Lori. She understood how much her daughter needed and loved the plump blond horse, which was why Tessa had held on to him for so long, even as she struggled to make ends meet. She had only sold him to help Lori, to protect the farm and her future. But she knew such changes were difficult and that Lori had been as brave and understanding as she could have possibly been—until Billy got lost in the wilderness.

Lori had done a bad thing by running away to find him, but she'd had good intentions. If Lori had just asked for help, her mother would have joined in her search—just as she was now.

"Where is my daughter's horse?" Tessa cried as she jumped out of her rental car at the edge of the ghost town. On Main Street, dozens of crew members were gathered, poring over maps of the desert. In the middle of the huddle were Fred and Blue. They sat in an electric all-terrain vehicle, with thick tires, the seats mounted up high. It was fitted with hand controls and a harness so Fred could drive, and there was a special seat for Blue beside him, plus a passenger seat behind.

Fred was holding a megaphone, calling out orders to the crowd. "I know everyone is tired, but we can't give up hope. I want us to divide into four groups; you will fan out into four quadrants of the Mojave, east, west, north, south. I want everyone to make sure their radios are powered up, since there's no cell service out there, and everyone in the Billy search party *must* go with a buddy. I don't want to have to send another search party out for *you* after we find this runaway horse!"

"And what about my daughter, Lori?!"

Fred stopped short at the sight of a woman barreling toward him through the dust, fear on her face.

"Oh my word, you're Tessa! It's me, Fred, Fred Narang." He raked a hand through his hair fitfully. "The park police told me Lori was missing, but when she didn't turn up here on set, I thought that meant you'd found her," Fred explained. "I've been looking forward to meeting you in person, but I sure wish it weren't under these circumstances. Tessa, you must be worried sick." Before she could reply, he turned back to the megaphone.

"New orders, team," he said to the gaggle of film crew members, the camera crane operator, the actors, the prop makers, the costumers, and more, all now a search party. "Billy can thrive on the wild bush muhly and fluff grass out here. He can chill with the donkeys if he finds a herd. We can let him hang out a little longer before we wrangle him back home." He looked at Tessa, who was wavering with fatigue and fear. "But for a seventh grader, the desert is a dangerous place," Fred continued. "So, it's all hands on deck: fan out and find Lori."

No one realized that there was one person missing from the search party: Marlowe Narang. In fact, he was close by and could hear every word from where he sat, just behind the swinging doors of the old saloon set. The room was staged for a scene, but filming had been suspended for the search. A table laid with props for a dinner was perfectly set in the middle of the room; cameras on tripods stood gathering dust in the corners. Flies buzzed over the meal that had been abandoned there by the actors because of the emergency, zipping around a bowl of fruit in the growing desert heat.

Marlowe had holed himself up in there away from the news cameras, police, and volunteers, at a loss for what to do. He read the headlines about the disaster on his phone and followed the Pony Tales social media group for updates, but mostly he just hid. He didn't want to look anyone in the eyes, he was so full of shame. He felt responsible for the runaway horse; if Marlowe hadn't "discovered" him on the stage at Lincoln Center, hadn't insisted the Fjord horse be his costar and brought him to this set underneath the Castle Mountains on the other side of the country, the yellow horse would still be safe. Billy wouldn't be alone, scared, lost in the wilderness, threatened by mountain lions and cactus spikes and who-knew-what-else out there among the black lava rocks and the prickly pears. Marlowe, who had no friends, had lost another.

Of course, no one could have predicted this disaster, and in reality, Marlowe was blaming himself unfairly. Blue had tried to tell him that. She was his dad's service dog, but they'd grown up together, and he was part of her pack now. And she knew the young boy was suffering. She'd tried her best to cheer him up. She waggled her tail at him and slurped him with her big pink tongue. She even flopped her body across his lap as he sat cross-legged, his head slumped in a corner of the saloon earlier that morning. But he had just pushed her off gently. Though she whined and thumped her tail on the ground, all her efforts to tell him he was loved and it was OK and no one blamed him—in the way a dog could, at least—didn't reach him.

And then he heard Tessa's words over the swinging double door. He gasped. *No one had told him a girl was missing too*. His father had not told him who had owned Billy. Even worse, Marlowe had not bothered to ask.

Her name is Lori. He was sick to his stomach. He had loved acting because of how he made people feel when he smiled, when he cried, when he laughed, when he scowled. His viewers felt his emotions along with him, and that brought them joy. That had brought his mother joy. He provided security for his father and adventure for the pair of them and Blue as they went all over the world from film shoot to TV studio. But in chasing that thrill, he hadn't stopped to think that the horse he wanted from the stage might have another kid who loved Billy too. Marlowe was dizzy with distress. In his mind, it was *his* acting career that had put a horse and a human in harm's way.

A quiet horror filled him. More than that, in taking another kid's horse, Marlowe had done something his mother, Fatima, would never, ever approve. He had taken away someone's dream.

He couldn't stand the feeling of powerlessness. He was Marlowe Narang, the Kibble Kid. *He could sell dog food to a cat*, for crying out loud! He made people happy for a living. That was the most important thing to him in the world. He stood up from his slump and pulled on his sneakers. Then he grabbed a cloth satchel from a pile of props in a corner and snatched some fruit before the desert bugs had their way with it. Five Granny Smith apples.

"Life is about helping others realize their dreams too."

His mother's words echoed through the empty saloon as if Fatima had spoken from the past. "Lori, I'll find your Billy."

The double doors creaked slightly when he swung them open slowly and crept onto Main Street. Amid the hubbub of milling reporters and volunteers at the other end of the ghost town, the black Labrador flicked her sensitive ears at the sound. The search party was busy filling up water bottles at a fountain near the actors' trailers, prepping for the hunt in the Mojave heat. Marlowe quietly walked in the opposite direction, slinking around the back of the battered buildings and down an alley. The sandstone spires of the Castle Mountains, the rust-red crags and bronze wasteland, unfolded before him. The Joshua trees looked like gnarled claws reaching out for him. He glanced behind him once to see that he had not been spotted by the crew, who would surely stop the actor from going on such a dangerous expedition all by himself. Then the most famous child star in the world vanished into the twenty million acres of the Mojave Desert.

Only Blue saw him go.

Chapter 14

HOOFPRINTS

"Astonishing," Lori said, her voice echoing a little off the black lava rocks beside the trail.

"That's an adjective. It means 'extremely impressive, amazing,'" Aiyana replied. The trio picked their way between the honey mesquite shrubs and their pricking spines and the catclaw acacias, called wait-a-minute bushes because of their tendency to tangle passersby in their thorns. They'd been out for hours now, practicing for Aiyana's quiz and searching for Billy. Only one of those things was going well.

No sign of Billy.

"Nice job. Now try 'adulation,'" Lori said. Sǫ-Sǫ was a pro at navigating the underbrush, stepping deliberately and gingerly, barely jostling the two girls on his back. Aiyana had put on a bareback pad, a few thick square blankets affixed with a cinch, not a saddle, so the two could ride comfortably together. A canteen hung from a carabiner by her knee.

"That's another noun," Aiyana said. "It means 'excessive praise.'"

"OK, 'appall,'" said Lori. Aiyana sat in front, steering, and Lori behind, motivating Sǫ-Sǫ every so often with a gentle bump on his flanks with her long legs. She easily sent him into an easy jog, what English riders call a trot.

"A spotted horse, short for 'Appal-oosa, the best kind of horsie there is!'" Aiyana giggled at her joke. Lori snorted. "I'm kidding; I know that one too," Aiyana said. "'Appall,' 'to horrify or greatly dismay.'"

That word felt apt to Lori right then as the sun settled into the hills. The desert was so vast, so wide, and Lori was so far from home. Her mother must be *appalled* at her daughter's reckless behavior. The word bounced around her mind, and she thought about how her mother had always been there for her; even when times were hard, even when her court cases ran late, and her clients demanded her attention, she always made time for Lori. And now Lori had ignored her in her moment of greatest worry. A knot of shame clenched in Lori's tummy. As the trio stepped through the scrub brush, Lori reached into her pocket and pulled out her phone. It was time to call her mom and tell her what she was up to. Maybe even ask, as Lori should have all along, for help.

There was no cell phone service out among the boulders and sand.

Lori tapped her friend on her shoulder. "I think we should turn back. You have your test to rest up for, and, well, I'm basically a fugitive. I think we should go get some grown-ups to help. I really have to call my mom." Aiyana sighed and nodded. She was *so* keen on finding the missing Fjord horse and maybe even meeting the Kibble Kid! But she knew Lori was right. She reluctantly lifted the reins in one hand and gently moved her hand to the right. It was a type of steering called neck-reining, which was used in Western riding. It was very different than what Lori knew, which was holding a rein in each hand to guide the horse, left to go left, right to go right. At the pressure of the leather on the opposite, left side of his neck, Sǫ-Sǫ expertly turned to the right. "You're right. Though I'm *appalled* we haven't found your horse."

As the Appaloosa pivoted back toward home, Lori cast her eyes down glumly. All those hours, all those miles, still no Billy. That was when she saw them: hoofprints in the sand. She tugged at Aiyana's shirt-sleeve and pointed. For a moment her heart raced, but then she deflated: They were tiny half-moons, not the saucer-sized hoofprints of a Norwegian Fjord horse. They beat a path that seemed to go right through a tall rock face. There were hundreds of them. All small. "Not him," Lori breathed out, her chin trembling.

"Lori, you know how you and I found each other? How you understood me, and I understood you, and now we are on the back of my horse traipsing around the desert, and when you go home, we are going to be pen pals and friends for the rest of our lives *no ifs, ands, or buts about it*?" Lori grinned and nodded. Aiyana was right about that, for sure. "That's because we are members of the same herd." Sitting in the back, Lori reached around Aiyana's waist and hugged her in thanks. "Well, Lor, those are wild donkey prints, a whole *herd* of them. Horses and donkeys are built similarly: They all feel good and safe when they are together. My auntie Tallulah taught me that they always find their herd. Like we found each other." She gripped the reins tighter. "Lori, I bet Billy found his herd too."

The girls knew just what to do without exchanging another word. Aiyana shifted her hand left this time.

Sǫ-Sǫ spun back around. Lori pressed her heels into his side. The Appaloosa burst into a lope. The trio galloped off down the trail of hoofprints.

What they didn't notice in their haste was that among the half-moons of the burros' hooves was a different fresh print.

Sneakers.

Sǫ-Sǫ's hooves clattered on scree and thudded in the dust. He could scent the burros in the distance, and his cattle ranching days came back to him in a rush. Being ranch trained, he spent years wandering across the horizon beneath a cowgirl or cowboy, searching for wayward steer and pushing them home. Now he dodged and ducked around prickers and scrub brush, his old cow horse–self coming alive. The girls gripped his back with their legs as he charged. On the heels of the wild donkeys, his mind filled again with the mission that once had been his life: Round up the herd. Lori wrapped her arms around Aiyana's waist, and her friend clung to Sǫ-Sǫ's mane. He rounded a bend and blasted between two rock faces, heading down a narrow passage without slowing. He may have been pokey when it came to running barrels at home, but here, on the heels of his quarry, the horse could not be stopped.

The barreling trio almost trampled Marlowe Narang.

"Whoa! Whoa!" the boy yelled, throwing up his hands as the Appaloosa shied sideways to avoid him. Aiyana almost fell off, gripping the horse's multicolored mane for stability. Lori *did* fall off. She slid almost in slow motion, her long legs gripping around the horse's barrel until they could no longer hold on. She fell lightly to the earth—thankfully unharmed.

Marlowe dashed across the path and ran over to her. She was already dusting herself off and shakily standing up. "Are you OK?" he asked. She brushed off the sand from her trousers and was about to answer him when Aiyana squealed. Her shriek echoed up the rock face, above which the last of the sun was winking out. It was dusk. They had entered a canyon of some sort, and the echo made her trill sound like a rope line of Marlowe fans. It might as well have been.

"Oh my gosh! You're Marlowe Narang. Kibble Kid, it's you. I loooooooooove you. I have your dog food. Wait, that came out wrong." She was practically hyperventilating. Lori cut her off.

"You're *Marlowe*," she said, her eyes narrowing to slits. "You lost my horse."

Her words echoed in the great canyon. It was as finely tuned a place as Lincoln Center, but this amplifier was built by nature itself. Her words bounced back and forth in the growing darkness like the maestro's booming voice across the theater, accusation after accusation with each repetition on the sandstone walls.

Marlowe had no response. So this was Lori. And he had not made her happy; he had caused her pain. He wanted to say, *"I'm so sorry, I didn't mean for this to happen"* or *"I've walked across the desert for an entire day, desperately trying to find him for you. My feet are sore, and my eyes sting from crying, but I've been trying, trying very, very hard, to make it right. I'm so sorry I stole your dream!"*

But instead, Marlowe saw in her eyes the ugly reflection of what she believed him to be. She had spoken aloud the words—the unkind, untrue words—that were in his own heart.

Instead, he sat down in the dust and sobbed.

Half a mile away, a black Lab's ears pricked up.

Chapter 15

GRANNY SMITH

The Fjord horse followed the swishing tails of the burros for miles and miles. They were kindly to him, and when they showed him their shoulders, he followed comfortably. He'd always eaten alfalfa and oats back in Springs. While the desert forage was tougher and chewier, it was yummy enough. As Billy walked among them, he scented a bobcat den hidden in a cranny of red rock and the trail of a coyote along the path, but he didn't panic. There was safety among the herd. He let the burros' funny whisk-broom tails flick the flies from his nose as he strolled amid them. He quickly developed a following of young donkeys.

They jostled for a place behind his rump because Billy expertly kept the gnats away from their faces with his lustrous, swishing tail.

As the herd grazed across the sizzling landscape, every so often Billy pulled his head up from the sagebrush to scan the horizon. He was looking for his Lori. *Was that her?!* No, it was the shadow cast from a piñon pine. He put his muzzle back down in the scraggly leaves and ripped them with his teeth.

Back in New York City, in the glow of the glitter of Lincoln Center, in the applause rising from the red velvet seats, and then in the hubbub of the movie set, the little horse had lost his way. When he had been swept up in *adulation*, he had almost forgotten his Lori. Now lost in the desert, he had actually found his path again: He realized that what had charmed him, what had made his chest swell and the crest of his two-tone mane arc with pride, was not *celebrity*. It was the feeling of mattering to others. Among the donkeys and the sand, he had time to think. It was there that he realized this fact: He had *already* been very important. To a girl who was his best friend in the world.

He had to find her. The herd of donkeys plus one Norwegian Fjord horse moved constantly, foraging from the meager Mojave blooms. Out in the wilderness, teams of cast members and crew, park rangers, groups of Pony Tales volunteers, and three seventh graders were looking for a horse hidden among the wild descendants of the cave-mining burros. The animals did not know this. They were not actually trying to hide, just find food, but as they kept pushing on through the Mojave, they stayed out of human reach. Horses eat for sixteen hours a day and can never feel full! They have to keep grazing as much as possible to supply the necessary nutrients to their big bodies. In his stall, Billy got tossed flakes of hay three times a day. Out in the wilderness, finding enough to eat was a full-time job.

He lifted his muzzle up again. *Lori?* No, a salt cedar, its branches flung out like arms, growing windblown on a crag. A donkey nipped him on the flank—keep moving, she said, in equine—and Billy trotted forward down a narrow path. Each hoof step echoed up the sides of the canyon wall so that he sounded like a whole herd of Fjords.

Around a bend in the rock, unaware of the herd of donkeys rambling through the scrub, Marlowe still sat in a slump. The Appaloosa stepped gently to him and dipped his nose down to where the actor sat. Sǫ-Sǫ breathed out a huff of air. It ruffled the boy's hair. Marlowe looked up into a polka-dot snoot.

The boy had been inconsolable, the girls at a loss as to what to do for him. Aiyana dismounted and thought about her angry days when she had not been the type of person horses and people could trust. She remembered when lashing out in anger in the moment felt like the only thing to do, but doing so never solved anything. She wanted to protect her friend from making the same mistakes she had, so she spoke gently. Giving feedback on someone's behavior can be difficult to do, but it is essential for true friendship.

"That was a little harsh, to accuse him of losing Billy," Aiyana said quietly to Lori. "He's out here in the desert also, all by himself; that's gotta mean he's real worried about Billy too. I'm sure he didn't mean for this to happen. And look how sad he is—he must feel terrible."

Lori was unmoved at first. "He's an actor. Can't they cry on cue?"

It was the Appaloosa who made Lori realize she was wrong. He began to snuffle Marlowe's neck. Sǫ-Sǫ, like all horses, was sensitive to distress. It reminded her of when Billy blew his sweet breath into her shoulder as she hugged him after a tough day at school or just stood there quietly in his stall and let her lean on him when she felt overwhelmed. Marlowe reached up a hand and stroked the soft spotted fur of Sǫ-Sǫ's long neck. He tangled his hands in the two-tone mane. His crying faded to sniffles. The horse peered at him through his starry blue eyes. He lipped at the boy's hair. Horses are always true. Horses never act. Sǫ-Sǫ knew Marlowe was not acting.

"I'm sorry, Marlowe," Lori said, kneeling beside the boy. Just a few days ago she would never have wanted a kid like this to notice her; she would have stepped away from any conflict, any problem, just to stay out of sight. Now she put her hand on his shoulder. "I know you didn't mean for this to happen. I'm just so upset."

He looked up at her through puffy eyes. "It is my fault; you're right. I just saw him onstage, in the limelight, and he filled me with a sense of—"

Lori finished the sentence. "Confidence," she said.

"Exactly." Marlowe sniffed.

"That's his specialty," Lori said. "And I'm actually kinda glad he can share that with other people too," she added.

"With his herd," Aiyana said quietly.

That was the gift all horses give. Sǫ-Sǫ had shared his gallop and his snuffly breaths that lifted spirits, just like Billy gifted his quiet strength to an awkward girl and a celebrity lost in more ways than one.

It was chilly now. The sun had set completely. There was no moon. The only light came from stars that shone as bright as the twenty-one starburst chandeliers that glittered over the stage at the Metropolitan Opera. The three kids there in the desert were totally, utterly lost. But there, at that moment, they somehow felt found. They had found their herd.

"I don't think it's safe to look anymore, or even turn back, until morning," Aiyana said. "Man, I'm gonna be in trouble." She began uncinching the girth holding the saddle blankets to Sǫ-Sǫ's back. "We can kind of rest on this to make the rocks less lumpy," she said, laying the cloth across the still-sun-warmed sandstone. She unclipped the canteen, and they began to pass it around and take careful sips of the water inside so as to not run out.

"Anyone hungry?" Marlowe rummaged into his prop satchel and pulled out the five green apples he'd lifted from the set. Aiyana took one and held her hand flat, tucking in her thumb carefully as she fed it to Sǫ-Sǫ. He ate it in two bites, crunching happily. The three humans leaned back on the blanket rolls and bit into their own. The sound of their chewing echoed up the sheer sandstone, each crunch reverberating into the dark Mojave night. In fact, the sound seemed to get louder and louder.

That wasn't crunching!

Clop-clop-clop-clop-clop-clop!

The canyon fairly shook with the sound of hoofbeats. They thundered over the stone and up the walls and then danced back and forth between them. Hundreds of hooves? Thousands of hooves? Were *a million* equines galloping headlong through the canyon in the dark to trample them where the three kids lay in the path? The Appaloosa trumpeted out a thin whinny. *Who goes there?* the timid neigh seemed to say in horse. Marlowe, Aiyana, and Lori jumped up, and the approaching hoofbeats clattered to a stop.

In the starlight, they saw the outline first. A soft muzzle, a spiky mane. Saucer-sized hooves, tufted ears. And then, the shape drew closer. In the faint starshine, it looked like a figure of gold, the same rich gold as the velvet curtain of Lincoln Center. The trio stood stock-still, unable to move, in shock. The creature trotted right up to Lori. It peered through the night, first with one eye, then with the other.

And let out wild, bugling *WHINNY*!

Lori was too stunned to speak. Billy ate the last Granny Smith apple right out of her hand.

Chapter 16

THE LAST RIDE

They awoke at dawn to the baying of a black Labrador retriever. Her howls resounded across the canyon. Blue had found them! She nosed all over the seventh graders, waking them up from where they lay curled on lumpy saddle blankets. She barked again and again. Billy and Sǫ-Sǫ pricked their ears at her. Blue wagged her tail.

Hot on her heels came the rumble of an ATV, growling across the stone. Fred Narang was in the driver's seat, and seated behind him was Tessa Allegria. She could barely contain herself when she saw her daughter. She pulled at the straps of her harness to unbuckle it and leapt from the vehicle almost before it came to a stop. She ran across the rocks and enfolded Lori in her arms.

"Mama, I'm so sorry, I'm so happy to see you, I'm so—I'm so—!" Lori's tongue got tied up in her emotions. Mother and daughter had their arms wrapped around each other, forgiveness and apology vibrating back and forth. Lori could muster only one word: "How?"

Fred answered instead. "Aiyana's aunt Tallulah saw her post on that Pony What'sit website," he said. "She's spent the entire night at the park rangers' headquarters, helping geo-locate you kids via Aiyana's phone." He turned to Aiyana. "She hasn't slept a wink with the worry you put her through, young lady." Aiyana looked down at her shoes and wrung Sǫ-Sǫ's reins in her hand. "We got ourselves close to Tallulah's coordinates in my ATV but couldn't spot you in the dark. Then Blue here just took off after a scent—Marlowe's as much her guy as I am—and led us to you." Marlowe stooped to wrap the Labrador in his arms.

"Good girl," the boy whispered in her soft floppy ear. "Goodest girl."

Tessa still held Lori to her. She reached out to Aiyana and drew the other girl close too. Aiyana hugged her back; it felt good to be found. Fred rummaged in a pack next to the driver's seat and pulled out PB&J sandwiches and juice boxes, which each of them gratefully took. "Kids, there will be consequences, but what matters most to all of us is that you and these animals are all safe and sound," Tessa said as they munched, slipping the crusts to the two cheerful horses. They glugged water from a canister emptied into a pail the grownups had brought, and one by one each horse gratefully slaked his thirst. "Now it's time to mount up on those horses. We have a lot of miles to cross to get us all home."

Home. Lori wondered what that meant the whole ride back to the *Once Upon a Horse* set. Aiyana's aunt would be waiting for her with her two-horse trailer to take her and Sǫ-Sǫ back to Bullhead City, she was sure, and Lori felt a pang that her new friend's home was not near hers. Marlowe's home was on the road, at whatever movie set or TV studio he was shooting at. Would she ever see these members of her herd again?

And Billy?

Aiyana and Marlowe rode Sǫ-Sǫ double in front of Lori, trailing the ATV, Marlowe wearing a motorcycle helmet his dad had pulled from a hatch in the vehicle. Lori steered him with the leadrope Aiyana had brought clipped to his dusty halter. But she barely needed to; he wanted to follow his herd home. The smokey tips of his ears framed the Mojave. His soft yellow fur took on the hue of the desert stretched before her.

No matter where they were, together felt like home.

But the Fjord horse was still technically Marlowe's. Legally, Billy's home was there on the set. Maybe it was enough, Lori reasoned, to know that a creature or a person you loved was safe and cared for. You don't have to *have* a horse to be a horseperson. Or even have ever ridden a horse. You just have to love them with passion in your heart. That was true for Lori; she loved the tubby blond horse with all her soul. And if you love a horse, some part of it stays yours, and some part of you stays theirs, forever.

Still, as they strode around the cacti and over the sandstone of Nevada, a far cry from the green-and-brown woods of Springs, Lori wished this ride on her beloved horse would never end, for it might be her last.

"Bravo! Bravo! *Bravo!*" The roar went up from the cast and crew as the group rounded a stand of Joshua trees hours later. The kids and horses had arrived at the ghost town, the ATV buzzing ahead to herald their return. Aiyana's aunt Tallulah burst from the crowd, tears streaming down her face, and the girl slipped from atop the Appaloosa to hug her. Seconds later Aiyana was chatting with her mother and father on her aunt's phone. She reassured them she was all right and promised over and over to never again strike out anywhere, particularly into the desert, without adult permission—even if it was a "horse emergency."

That night, there was a festive dinner in the old saloon on set, catered by Auntie Tallulah from her Navajo food cart. The three new friends were merry, but each had accepted that after this night, they would be very grounded. For *a while*. Marlowe had agreed to walk Blue for a month straight, and Aiyana and Lori said they would both take extra shifts mucking stalls before *and* after school at their respective barns. (Not that any of them minded more time with the animals!)

At the head of the table, Fred had parked his wheelchair beside Tessa and they sat together joking and chatting. They were joyful with relief, but Blue the Labrador could tell they were joyful with something else too. After that first phone call about Billy months earlier, when they'd chatted well past midnight, Fred found himself calling Tessa to arrange the horse's travel plans and then for no reason at all. Tessa had rung him back to finalize details and then sometimes just to tell him about her day. The first time they met in person was on set, climbing into Fred's ATV to search for Lori. As they looked high and low for her, Fred's radio crackled; it was the director: Marlowe had gone missing too! During their search for the children they loved, stricken with worry, the minutes turned to hours. As the hot sun roasted the tops of their heads and then the Mojave night chilled their bones, the two grown-ups had shared their fears and their dreams. Fred spoke about how he had always wanted to help run an equine therapy center to give other disabled people the gift of bravery that horses had given him. Tessa shared her dream of creating a refuge in Springs for people who needed the safe space horses gift us, like her daughter, Lori, found in their barn.

Laughing with relief, surrounded by the three children, the horses safely stabled nearby, the grown-ups' shared dreams seemed to swell across the twenty million acres of the Mojave. Smiling bashfully, Tessa and Fred clasped hands atop the table. Beneath the table, Blue thumped her tail.

"We have an announcement." It was Auntie Tallulah speaking. She clinked her knife against her glass for attention. The saloon was packed. Actors, extras, film crew, park rangers, and even Pony Tales volunteers from Arizona, Nevada, and California who had helped with the search spilled out the swinging doors into the dirt main street of the ghost town. There were reporters there, too, ready to tell the story of the disappearing horse, the missing child star, the runaway girls, and the herd they became. They all put down their fry bread and readied their notebooks and microphones to report whatever was about to be said.

"There has been a casting change for *Once Upon a Horse*, the movie," Auntie Tallulah announced. *How strange*, Marlowe thought, since Auntie Tallulah wasn't part of the cast or crew. Her catering was scrumptious, but what say did she have in casting *his* movie? He shot a glance at his father, who shushed Marlowe with a shake of his head.

Oh no, Marlowe thought. Had his stunt meant he was being kicked out of the cast? A pang hit his stomach, and he felt the room swim. In the theater at Lincoln

Center, in his itchy tuxedo, he had been ready to ditch acting—ready to leave it behind because over the years he had taken for granted all the fun, all the delight, all the adventure he once got from performing. He had grasped to get that joy back on this very set. Oh no. Was he now going to get what he wished for at the opera? Was his acting career about to end? What a terrible moment to realize, too late, how much he actually loved what he did!

"The most important role in this film will now be played by a performer who *loves* to perform." *That's me!* Marlowe thought. Beside him at the table, Lori saw the pain and loss on Marlowe's face. She was desperate to defend him. He had snuck off his set, disrupted filming, put himself—and the teams of search parties—in danger. But it had not been because he didn't care; it had been because he loved Billy. And because he wanted *her*, a stranger then, to be happy. For Lori to have her dream.

She grabbed Aiyana's hand beside her at the table. The girl from Bullhead City turned and looked the girl from Springs in the eyes. Like horses, the girls didn't need words to communicate. Aiyana's gaze said back to Lori: *I am here for you*. And so, Lori did what was once unthinkable. There, in front of more than a hundred people, with national television and radio news reporters embedded in the crowd and listening to every word, Lori spoke up.

"Marlowe Narang *is* the star of this film," Lori said, and the whole room turned to her. "He is my friend. He is a very talented actor. And he is an even better person."

The room was silent for a moment. Tallulah remained where she stood, a quizzical look on her face. Then she resumed speaking. "You're very right about that, Lori, and I want to thank you for sharing," she said. "But Marlowe is *not* the star of this film." Lori sucked in a breath to protest again, but Tallulah raised her hand for silence. Lori took a sip of water to still the many things this once-silent girl wanted to say in support of her new friend.

"My horse Sǫ-Sǫ is."

Chapter 17

THE STAR

The water sprayed out of Lori's mouth in a startled splutter. She was too shocked to be embarrassed.

"*What?!*" yelled Marlowe, Aiyana, and Lori at exactly the same time.

Fred spoke next. "I discussed with the director, and Sǫ-Sǫ's owner, Tallulah, and it seems that this leopard Appaloosa is a natural star." Aiyana squeaked. She couldn't lose Sǫ-Sǫ! Fred smiled at her. "It helps that he lives nearby and can remain at home, under the care of his favorite girl while shooting. I hear she has learned to be very gentle, and the horses love her." Aiyana applauded wildly.

Tessa turned to Lori, and only then did daughter notice mother holding Fred Narang's hand, her eyes smiling brightly. Her mother spoke now: "And there's one more casting change, hon. Our Billy has a very important new job. He is so good, and so brave, and so generous that I believe he will make a perfect therapy horse at the new therapeutic riding center I plan to convert our stables into back in Springs." Lori was floored. She'd set out across the country to find Billy, to make sure he was safe. She hadn't dared to dream she could bring him home!

Her heart raced. But how could they afford to buy back their horse? Billy's sale had saved the farm and more. As amazing as it would be to have him home, Lori felt she could not let her mother suffer more on her behalf. Tessa seemed to guess her question. "The Narangs have generously donated him. Actually, it was discussions with Fred while we were out in the ATV trying to do something other than worry ourselves sick over you kids that inspired the new program," she said. "Billy will head back with us to Springs tomorrow."

Fred smiled up at Tessa from his wheelchair, his eyes full of pride. And something more. "And Marlowe and Blue and I will be coming to visit. A lot."

As the party wrapped up, the cast and crew headed to bed in their trailers, and the news trucks sped off to file their reports, their wheels kicking up dust as they buzzed off through the desert. And the three seventh graders stepped out into the chilly Mojave night. They went to visit the horses stabled under a blue-and-white tent at the edge of the ghost town. Bright klieg lights were trained on the yucca and brittlebushes this time to keep any curious mountain lions at bay. A guard was posted up in a pickup truck as an extra safety precaution. The three kids leaned over the slats of the stall. They rubbed the forelocks of the tubby Norwegian Fjord and the lanky Appaloosa and told them what good boys they were.

Out in the distance, they could hear the hee-*haw* of a herd of wild burros passing through the night. Billy wondered if his fan club of young donkeys was missing him. Then he snuffled Lori's neck and realized he had everything he needed right there.

"We're all going to stay connected," Lori said after a while. "Sǫ-Sǫ will be on set, and so will you, Aiyana, so you'll see Marlowe all the time, since he's still the human star. And your dad and my mom"—Lori blushed, and the others giggled—"seem to *like*-like each other . . . so we'll be back and forth, too, I imagine." Aiyana smiled, scritching Sǫ-Sǫ under his chin, and his lips curled a little, a horse's chuckle. "And actually"—Lori couldn't believe she was saying this—"I was wondering, Marlowe, if maybe I could be an extra on *Once Upon a Horse*? I've had this dream to try out performing. Got any parts for a really tall girl?"

Marlowe stared at her, eyes wide in surprise, then began nodding furiously. "Anyone have a scrap of paper? I can write one!" Their laughs echoed into the desert dark.

"We'd be connected anyway," Aiyana said.

"Yeah," Marlowe chimed in, tilting his head back to look at the stars. They joined him in gazing at the great big universe flung out up above. "We're a herd."

Lori's gaze turned back to Billy, to the horse who had helped her find her voice and who, more importantly, had loved her just the same when she didn't have one. She couldn't wait to start training to become a certified therapeutic riding instructor. And she couldn't wait to show the fuzzy yellow horse with the inky stripe that there was another way to be important. A way that had nothing to do with cameras, stages, *adulation*, or applause. As a therapy horse, Billy would share the gift of his kindness, his goodness, and his bravery. From her pocket, she fished out a little doggy bag she'd grabbed from dinner and fed him a scrumptious Granny Smith slice.

He was going to be a star.

Author's Note

Billy is a real horse—a little yellow Norwegian Fjord—and he really did trot across center stage in *Aida* at the Metropolitan Opera in New York City's Lincoln Center! I know this because I was there in 2019, stage left, holding his bridle as the trumpets played and he waited for his trot-on part! For my nonfiction book for adults, *Horse Crazy: The Story of a Woman and a World in Love with an Animal*, I followed horses and the people who love them all around the globe, from the belly of a 747 full of warmbloods to behind the golden velvet curtain of my favorite place in the world—the opera! That is where I met the real-life Billy, who is owned by a grown-up named Lori Allegra and lives with her and her husband, John, at Allegra Farm in East Haddam, Connecticut.

But Once Upon a Horse, the series you're reading now, is a work of fiction—based on real life. So onstage in *Aida* is where the true story ends and the real fun begins: Billy's journey to the ghost town movie set is from my imagination, as are his friends Marlowe, Aiyana, Sǫ-Sǫ, and Blue. However, since I'm a reporter for the *New York Times* when I'm not writing about horses, I *really* love facts. That means everything from the kissing bugs to the Joshua trees to the history of the wild donkeys and Appaloosas you read in this book is absolutely real.

Unlike Lori, I've never had a problem speaking my mind, but I've overcome other challenges that you can read about in book one of the Once Upon a Horse series, *The Flying Horse,* which is based on my own life. Horses have always helped me through hard times. Now, I help horses help other people, by serving on the advisory board of the *real-life* GallopNYC, a nonprofit therapeutic riding stable in New York City, where the fictional character of Fred Narang learns to ride and thrive.

Acknowledgments

Thank you to my editor, Summer Dawn Laurie; Amy Novesky for being horse crazy too; and to Lauren Reischer, head coach of the inaugural Special Olympics New York Equestrian Show Team, GallopNYC rider, and tireless advocate for equestrians with disabilities like her. She made sure I got it right.

And to all the horses and riders at GallopNYC— you are stars.

SARAH MASLIN NIR is a reporter for the *New York Times*, a Pulitzer Prize finalist, and the author of *The Flying Horse* and *The Jockey & Her Horse*, the first two books in the Once Upon a Horse series. She is also the author of the adult memoir, *Horse Crazy: The Story of a Woman and a World in Love with an Animal*. Second only to Sarah's love of horses, which she has been riding since the age of two, is her love of horse books. *The Star Horse* is her third novel for young readers. She lives in New York City.

LAYLIE FRAZIER, a fine artist and illustrator who lives in Houston, Texas, created the spot art for this book. Laylie doesn't ride horses, but she loves to illustrate them.